Unlicensed Travel

Inter-Planetary Alliance

Will Soulsby-McCreath

For all of us who love our families even when it's hard.
And those of us who left and built our own Ahthae.

Content Warning:

References to people trafficking, scenes of consensual intimacy, personal impact of the loss of a culture, and people struggling with familial relationships.

A quick note about language and pronouns:

If you are unfamiliar with neo-pronouns, they do appear in this novel. In particular you'll come across the singular they, as well as others like ey, eir, em and xe, xyr, xem.

As with the first book, Unlicensed Delivery, this book is written from the perspectives of characters whose primary language of communication is a fictionalized future language. Most of it matches modern British English, which is entirely because that's the language I write my books in.

I wanted to make it accessible but still futuristic, so most of the words I've chosen to include are similar enough to their English counterparts that it shouldn't take too much working out. That is, apart from aufenthaltsraum, which is a German compound word created for me by a lovely writer I met online.

Aufenthaltsraum

– Ow-Fen-Thal-ts-Room – A "Spending Time Room" –

A room whose designated purpose is for use as relaxation in all its forms. Can include sections for botany, cooking, crafting, eating, lounging, gaming, vids, etc.

Also By
Will Soulsby-McCreath

The Guardian Cadet Series
Merry Arlan: Breaking The Curse
Merry Arlan: Finding The Heir
Kitty Hughes: An Unexpected Meeting (short story)

Welcome To Humanity

Inter-Planetary Alliance Novels
Unlicensed Delivery
Unlicensed Travel

Not That Kind Of Dandy
Not The Fighting Kind
Not The Fainting Kind
Not That Kind Of Dandy Omnibus

Unlicensed Travel

Inter-Planetary Alliance Novels
2

Will Soulsby-McCreath

Prologue

**Messages from
Sauraxen of Pitzk
to
Pitzk: Sau.
Collected by Ratch on PT75-
129.
Transcribed automatically for
longevity of record.
Request audio playback?**

*Sent from:
R1bb1t-MC4TS, SA.D1*

Hey vava.

So my life got a bit chaotic there and—do you remember Basti, my friend from uni? We roomed together, he was doing his captaincy Master's Degree while I was studying for my engineering one? He's finally bought that ship he always talked about. And he asked me to come on as his chief engineer, which I don't have to tell you is quite the promotion. Anyway, I decided to go for it so don't send any more messages to my old address, it's R1bb1t-MC4TS via Captain Sebastian LeaYaPar-Jones now.

The ship itself is a real clunker. Sturdy and solid, but somebody had a fun time personalising it a few years ago and now we all have to deal with the fallout of that. I love it. Best deal I ever got. Oh and Matter is here too—you remember Matter? I told you about meeting them at that fancy ambassadorial dinner where I was being trotted around like some pretty prize everybody needed to see and people kept trying to shake my hand, hate that. Matter found me hiding in a cupboard when they went to hide in a cupboard. Anyway, they're the pilot, which is awesome because Matter gives the best cuddles bar yours in the entire universe! They make anywhere feel like home.

We're doing our Deep Space Travel Assessment now, Secondary Assessment started today and I kinda hate that our assessor is a harrushetti because those guys are scary. But I can make it work. I've been in weirder situations. None come to mind, but I'm sure I have.

Anyway, I'll update you next time something fun or interesting happens.

Love, Sauraxen.

Sent from:
R1bb1t-MC4TS, SA.D15

Hi vava.

We found a stranded cryopod ship out in the void with a single person left alive on it. Her name is Chamber and apparently her people were at war with Ouaeahhn before the IPA even existed. Imagine that, Ouaeahhn at war! She might be the last of her kind in the universe. And she… well, she's mostly handling it okay except she cannot stand Matter. I get it, they're ouaeahhn and it reminds her of the war, but it's hard to be on a ship with someone who spends a lot of time disliking your friend's entire culture for something that happened before any of us can remember.

We ended up dropping her off at an IPA Station called Omega-Sethi—at her request, not just dumping her for making things tense. I have to admit, though, I definitely prefer the ship without her on it. That feels mean…

The assessor is still harrushetti—obviously, that's

not the kind of thing that can change—but he's not as bad as I first thought. He's quite… considerate really. And he knits and spends a lot of time taking care of the plants. It's kinda cute.

Anyway, that's all for now. Love you.

Sauraxen.

I.P.A.

Sent from:
R1bb1t-MC4TS, SA.D21

We finally got a job, vava!

We had to land on this weird place called EC.63, which is an Earth Colony. It's apparently got this really complicated history about crash landings and welcoming aliens but mostly it's just bright there. We only landed because I needed a junkyard to find a replacement piece for the kettle. You should have seen it when the assessor guy came in to request the replacement piece, he got his words all muddled up— ugh, it's hard to explain over voice notes that I know are going to be compressed into text files and played with that awful voiceover. The point is, we got a job. Transporting a thing called 'racattle snakes' to a few systems over. I can safely say I'd rather room with one of the harrushetti than spend any time with those beasts but as long as they stay out of engineering, I'll be fine.

Love you.

Sauraxen.

Sent from:

R1bb1t-MC4TS, SA.D23

The racattle snakes got out! There was one in engineering! I think this might be the most terrifying day of my entire life!

Sent from:

R1bb1t-MC4TS, SA.D24

The beasts are gone. Dropped off at their final destination. Some lab for study and care apparently. I don't know, it was really foggy there and I didn't want to go out with those creatures. I stayed safely tucked away in my room behind a door—which is like a wall but you can get rid of it whenever you want.

Sent from:
R1bb1t-MC4TS, SA.D25

Hi vava.

Sorry you got two dramatic messages in a row. Here's hoping they came through together and you didn't have to wait after I complained about the things getting out before you heard from me again.

In much nicer news, today is Matter's birthday! I've told you about birthdays before, they're a very human celebration of hatching day that you get every year. There's celebrations and presents and cake. I made them this bottle thing that's supposed to look like the sky out in space. I'm not sure how well it works, but they seemed happy with it. And Dimae— Basti's husband—made cake for everyone who could eat it.

Better yet we got to progress to our Tertiary Assessment, so that starts today or tomorrow. Oh shoot, I should probably explain that too. So Deep Space Travel Assessments come in three parts, a Primary Assessment on planet or station to assess your psychological readiness and capability for the dangers and stresses of regular deep space travel. Then a Secondary Assessment where you get to travel and be assessed as you go. And a Tertiary Assessment, which seems to be just the same as the Secondary one but longer? I dunno, there's probably something specific to it that I'm just oblivious to. You know me, if it's not circuit boards and engine parts I'm not paying attention.

Talk soon.

Sauraxen.

Sent from:
R1bb1t-MC4TS, TA.D5

Hi vava.

We got a job in a galaxy called Clickclick, which I think is probably the worst IPA translation I've come across. Specifically on a planet called Clicksphere. Basti actually asked me to go down on the planet with him. It was weird. They build tunnels above the ground. They were kinda rude about my clothes, which is ridiculous because I'm only wearing clothes for wider attitudes about appropriateness. I miss being around people who don't think nudity is a problem! Ugh and all they wanted us to transport was a single briefcase. It seems pointless, but Basti is going ahead with it so I guess we're going along with whatever.

Love, Sauraxen.

Sent from:
R1bb1t-MC4TS, TA.D7

The fucking emergency engine crapped out on us and we're still in Clickclick so there's no parts to replace it and Basti doesn't even understand why we have an emergency engine and I wish I'd never even joined this stupid crew!

Sent from:
R1bb1t-MC4TS, TA.D9

I didn't think our plight could get any worse but Basti got pulled in by Clickglobe—the planet we had to deliver that briefcase to—authorities for illegal cargo. Somehow we're the ones in trouble instead of the sender and they're extorting services out of us.

Sent from:
R1bb1t-MC4TS, TA.D11

Hi vava,

I'm sorry I keep sending you random unhappy messages. It's not as bad as all that, it's just sometimes I need someone to talk to who isn't on this crew. I could probably chat with someone in real time, like a friend on a planet or station but it's just nicer talking to you. I guess I am just a hatchling sometimes, wanting my vava even though I'm too much an adult to need one.

I managed to get parts to repair the emergency engine with—Basti almost tried to sell me in exchange due to translator error at the travelling marketplace, but that's more of a funny story since Matter came and fixed it all as per usual. We're still stuck in Clickclick on the job, but that's got to be over with soon. Then we can get out of here and onto more normal jobs.

Can't wait to hear back from you.

Sauraxen.

Sent From:
Station Gnarresh-Fle. IPA
Standard date 35JX243

Hi vava.

I can't believe I haven't heard back from you yet, it's been 24 days since I last sent something and I haven't got any replies yet. Is everything okay?

We had… It wasn't the best time ever. So, that

cargo we were extorted into carrying, that was illegal guns, which we only found out because Matter bumped into the crates and knocked one open. Basti reached out to the Clickclick authorities but they ended up being just as ridiculous as everyone else we met in that galaxy and made us carry the cargo until— I didn't know it at the time but we were waiting for pirates to board us like a sting operation. I'm still kinda mad at Basti about putting us through that, especially since, you know, we got boarded by pirates! I'm okay, obviously. This message would have started very differently if I wasn't.

It was scary there for a while though. The pirates disabled the entire ship and everyone got kinda hurt. And then we were just floating in space, no engines and no real hope of help. Again, we're fine. Matter did some snazzy ouaeahhn piloting to get us to Harrush— that's not a nice place, by the way, wouldn't recommend a visit. Everything is really bright because it's an ice planet, and cold too. And the people are ridiculously formal and seem to dislike outsiders, so that was a fun time. Especially since both of our harrushetti needed serious medical treatment so Matter, Basti, and I were just kind of abandoned there.

But everyone got better.

And now we're on an IPA Space Station called Gnarresh-Fle so we can go through *another* set of assessments because our Tertiary Assessment got interrupted and there isn't an IPA rule for this kind of situation so it'll probably be at least 100 days before anything happens.

Seriously, write me back, I'll be bored otherwise. And tell whoever it is that they're not going to the broadcast tower enough. I know this one is being sent from Gnarresh-Fle but it's probably best to send it to R1bb1t-MC4TS, Galactic Whale, via Captain Sebastian LeaYaPar-Jones so I'll get it even if we move on.

Love you.

Sauraxen.

Messages from
Sauraxen of Pitzk
to
Pitzk: Xanaka.
Collected by Ratch on PT75-129.
Transcribed automatically for

longevity of record.
Request audio playback?

Sent From Station Gnarresh-Fle. IPA Standard date 35JX243

Hi Xanaka, is everything okay?

I haven't heard back from vava for over 55 days, which is a bit long for it just to be between broadcast tower trips, isn't it? Message me back at R1bb1t-MC4TS, Galactic Whale, via Captain Sebastian LeaYaPar-Jones.

Please.

Sauraxen.

Sebastian

It wasn't that Inter-Planetary Alliance chairs were particularly or specifically uncomfortable. Not necessarily, it was just that they weren't exactly designed to fit Basti's body. The way the backrest was aligned, forcing him to either lean too far back, leaving him unbalanced, or sit up as if there were no backrest at all. The seat itself was too narrow for his body, designed to accommodate people with an extra pair of legs who would want to settle said legs on every side of the seat of the chair—perching on it more like a stool—as much as it was designed to fit people with a bodies a similar shape to Basti's. But, no, really the chair was fine. Basti was beyond used to IPA standardised chairs and their relative discomfort.

The problem, what had Basti squirming in the uncomfortable chair, was the situation. Basti was sat in a standardised office with no real personalisation to spot on the IPA grey walls or placed with care atop the IPA standardised desk, with a bureaucrat who had all the power over not just Basti but his crew as well.

It didn't matter that this bureaucrat had to be pretty far down the list of people in charge to be assigned to deal with Basti's problem; she was still an authority figure and she still set Basti's teeth on edge. Still had Basti squirming in his uncomfortable IPA chair. All made yet worse by the way she looked at Basti with her cat-like ears flat enough to balance a tray on top of. She thought she was debasing herself in some way by having to deal with Captain Sebastian LeaYaPar-Jones: human. Would this conversation— such as it was considering she hadn't said anything yet—have gone better if the bureaucrat wasn't one of the types of alien Basti was most familiar with? He had married a harrushetti, after all; he knew those facial expressions and subvocalisations intimately. Would it have been better if he couldn't read her face? Or would he have been just as anxious in the face of the unknown?

The silence stretched too long, Basti either had to move or speak. So he tried to keep himself from snapping when he asked, "Can you explain why it says provisional on my ship's Deep Space Travel License?" He didn't add the 'or not' that would be too rude. But considering he'd booked the meeting with her with the title 'provisional stamp on Deep Space Travel license' it was somewhat frustrating. He'd even done it in Harrushetti language and spelling—with a lot of help from Dimae.

"It says here," the bureaucrat gestured to her datapad, clawed hand swiping past the pronoun patch on her shirt, an embroidered piece in direct contrast to the rest of her formal and bland outfit.

It was rare for harrushetti to use she/her pronouns, their concept of gender not lining up with linguistic practices in wider IPA languages like Earth Common Eurean—not to mention the fact that most Harrushetti struggled to manage words that began with an 's'. But Basti wasn't actually about to start questioning someone else's pronouns.

"That your DST—" She pronounced it 'DeST' the way Dimae did, avoiding the S and making it into a single word. "—assessment was derailed by…" Her ear flicked, the little pink bow pierced through it dancing in the light and shining the same colour as her nose.

As she began to list the things that had gone wrong for the crew in the process of their Deep Space Travel assessment, Basti couldn't hold in his sigh. Trust the IPA to need each member of a crew to go through their licensing experience independently, only for them to end up judged as a group. But nobody said IPA rules made sense. They, like the chairs, had to fit as many forms as possible without the need for exceptions.

Exceptions like Basti's husband also being his doctor on a ship so small the crew comprised of only five people.

Exceptions like Matter being the one to reach out for help when everything had gone horribly wrong despite the fact that it was Sebastian's ship.

Exceptions like what the Clickclick authorities had insisted Basti do when he had tried to turn over the illegal weapons he had been threatened into taking aboard in the first place.

And none of that even began to address the issues that Basti hadn't considered important enough to include in his report until he'd asked if Brruuh intended to address them—since the cognitivist had started out as their DST license assessor before requesting to join the crew.

"That doesn't exactly lend itself to a full license," the bureaucrat concluded.

"I'm not debating what happened during the assessment," Basti argued. "It's more like an enquiry as to what the provisional designation means. Where we go from here. When I can expect to get rid of that stamp."

"The provisional designation requires your whole crew to be cleared by an independent IPA medical officer as fit for duty following their injuries, then you'll be scheduled a provisional license test. You can hardly expect to take an injured and unwell crew into

Deep Space when you don't know how far away from a medi-station you might find yourselves."

"I have a medical officer." Not an official requirement for needing a Deep Space Travel License, though it was generally accepted as good practice. No, according to IPA regulations there needed to be a captain, an engineer, a pilot, and one other crew member at the minimum. At least one of them had to have medical training, which was why Sebastian's MSc in Captaincy and Command had included a first aid module. He couldn't have afforded a doctor, could barely afford the rest of his crew. Basti had pulled in a lot of favours to wrangle the ship to functional and staffed. To have landed everyone in the position of being stuck in harrushetti space dragged at him like the gravity from a black hole.

"Irrelevant."

Basti held in a sigh. A question balanced on the tip of his tongue. One he wasn't sure he should ask. Matter hated to talk about it, hated drawing attention to it. But if an IPA medical officer had to clear them all for duty, that meant, as their captain, surely Sebastian had to raise it. "What about chronic illnesses?"

The bureaucrat flicked over the datapad, obviously shifting from page to page. But that information was locked behind a medical wall, and this IPA bureaucrat might be a lot of things, including in a mystery position since the text on her designation arm band was in Harrushetti, which Basti didn't read. But, by lack of symbol alone, she was not a medical professional.

Basti failed to hold in another sigh. If the IPA didn't have paperwork and systems in place already designated for a situation like that, it would mean a council meeting about the whole thing, and who knew how long that would take. He wasn't about to kick his pilot off the ship, even if they weren't also his sibling and his friend. He certainly wouldn't do it for something they could manage perfectly well and that wasn't even their fault.

Not to mention that would require leaving Matter stuck in the harrushetti-run galaxy for the foreseeable future, since Deep Space Travel was apparently disallowed for any of them until this provisional stamp stopped glittering over the top of all their licenses and IDs.

"And in the meantime?" Basti asked, all hope sinking deeper than his boots. Deeper than the deepest chasm in the chasm-ey-est planet he could think of.

"You're welcome to find jobs within the galaxy."

Right. Cargo running jobs in and around Harrush and Station Gnarresh-Fle. Those would be plentiful for a human captain with an alien crew! Because harrushetti were known for their benevolent and welcoming nature—oh wait, nope. Basti was barely allowed into his in-laws home because he was from a different planet, regardless of the fact that if he and Dimae split it would be putting Dimae's health at risk.

"How long will it take to start the new assessment?" Basti grit out.

"I couldn't hope to tell. We would need a qualified cognitivist and this station doesn't currently have any.

"Brruuh?" Basti offered, clinging to what little hope he could find, since Brruuh had already filled out the transfer paperwork to become a member of his crew.

The bureaucrat shook her head. Impartiality— supposed impartiality was important in harrushetti culture.

"Are you going to request one?" Basti asked, losing any semblance of the patience he'd been clinging to.

"It will take up to two IPA designated weeks to expect to hear a response, and up to an IPA designated year before we can expect to get anyone out here. And I cannot make the request until you crew have been cleared from medical leave—after all; we couldn't waste anyone's time."

His time, it seemed, wasn't valuable like anyone else's. Basti stood, swallowing back the angry words he wanted to hiss and spit at the bureaucrat. It wasn't her fault; she was just the unhappy face being plastered all over the problem. "Thanks for your time."

"Captain," she called before Basti could escape her office. "Your ship will need to be cleared before it leaves this station. The damage to it was extensive and we cannot have a vessel flying around that might break down, even within the galaxy."

Because harrushetti were very clean and tidy people. A clunker like the Galactic Whale breaking down in their orbital space would be an eyesore!

Brruuh

"**W**e're stuck here," Sebastian announced, launching himself into one of the dining chairs set around the table in the aufenthaltsraum with an emphasis that must have been painful. It reminded Brruuh of nothing so much as a kitten launching themself into a sulk. Emotions too large for the form that contained them.

"On the Station?" Matter asked, shifting in their lounge on the sofas next to Sauraxen and Brruuh but not quite making it to their feet. They pinged a hair tie from their wrist toward Basti, the way he caught it betraying a longstanding habit of such action. Siblings!

Basti started pulling his cloud of dark coils into its usual pineapple shape on the top of his head. "Kind of. We need the ship to clear harrushetti regs, but even then we're stuck in the galaxy until we get a new assessor to take the provisional stamp away."

"Does that mean we did a whole DST assessment just to get informally rejected?" Sauraxen asked.

"Basically," Sebastian huffed.

Brruuh ran a soft hand over her scales, announcing his departure before he shifted over to the coffee machine, setting it working. The normal undercurrent scent of coffee that spread over the whole ship and its crew had turned sharp with the frustration felt amongst said crew. If any of the more scent-focused species wanted to maintain focus, a covering scent would be useful, and every other meeting seemed to have a round of hot drinks. Was that a human habit? Or just a wider-Jones family habit?

"A provisional—" he paused, trying to think of a word to replace 'stamp' so he could avoid the difficulty of starting a word with an S. Since joining the crew of Galactic Whale officially, and their recent extended stay in Harrushetti space, Brruuh had come to discover other harrushetti didn't struggle with it as much as he did. Whether it was a YaBin trait, a kittenish trait he should have grown out of, or just Brruuh, he couldn't say. But avoiding it was an ingrained habit at this point. Would designation be the right word or...? "—badge is a little different," Brruuh explained.

He had handed out enough of those particular

stamps in his time working on Station Ana-Bay. Usually to crews that were falling apart from grief, or who hadn't considered the weight of inter-galactic travel. It was a stamp he might have been inclined to—had been inclined to cover Matter's file with when they had first met. Their cavalier attitude toward the inherent danger had been difficult to fathom, difficult to see as anything but negative. But after spending 121 days with them he had started to understand the way they interacted with the world more. Matter took the job seriously, it was life they made fun of. And bureaucracy.

This crew wouldn't have been given provisional status if not for the mismanagement in Clickclick, if not for the way they had blasted into harrushetti space in a broken down ship. It was clear to Brruuh— and anyone else with a brain—that the resourcefulness shown in the wake of such difficulty was a valuable trait allowed out into the depths of space.

"It's not a rejection, exactly," Brruuh explained. "More like a postponement, a request for further investigation." He sighed into the cupboard, trying to disguise it by pulling out his tin of eenya for him and Dimae, neither of whom could tolerate the caffeine in coffee.

This crew wouldn't get through a harrushetti level of further investigation. And the cognitivists who could offer such assessments were few and far between. Even Brruuh wasn't fully qualified for it. He could hand out provisional stamps, but getting them removed was above his level of qualification. Off the top of his head, he could ask Yarrun, or Talisa, and there was always Vedran, reluctant as Brruuh might be to reach out to Vedran after the birthday cake incident. But would harrushetti authorities allow someone Brruuh knew to perform the assessment? Talisa and Yarrun would never let friendship come in the way of their work; it was a large portion of the base of Brruuh's friendship with them. Glancing over at his lounging paramour, currently plaiting back her best friend's purple hair, he wondered idly if what he had with Yarrun and Talisa was even friendship. Were they just colleagues?

Either way, friendly colleague or legitimate friend, was it worth reaching out? Seeing if he could convince them to travel to Gnarresh-Fle? They might be willing, might travel faster than an official IPA request would get anyone out here.

"Does it matter whether it's a rejection or a postponement if we can't leave either way?" Matter asked.

Brruuh bristled but had no decent response. It was different to him. It mattered to him that there was a difference. But it also didn't make a difference to the crew in the greater scheme of it: it wouldn't be any easier to get a Deep Space Travel license rejection overwritten than it would be to get a provisional stamp removed. Not here in the depths of harrushetti space.

Of all the council members in the IPA, harrushetti were the ones who liked paperwork and planning and bureaucratic timelines the most. It was one of Brruuh's least favourite pieces of his home culture, even if he knew he followed those tendencies to a self-destructive extent.

He set the drinks on the table, carrying his, Sauraxen's and Matter's tucked into the crook of an arm, returning to the sofas. When Brruuh had first arrived, he hadn't approved of the layout of the aufenthaltsraum. Hadn't really approved of aufenthaltsraums at all. Brruuh would much rather have a room for each of the designations an aufenthaltsraum offered: a botany space, a kitchen and dining space, and a chilling out space. Aufenthaltsraums combined all the above and anything else the crew might need a space for. For Galactic Whale, the fact that the sofas faced the dining table had gone into Brruuh's initial report notes, *'blurring the lines between dining and relaxing'*. When he found Basti working in the space, running crew meetings here, he had disapproved even more.

But, after some time on the ship, after getting to know the crew a little better, he could see the way humans and wrexi both turned meetings on and off. They changed posture or shifted seats after a meeting had closed. Making designations of their own where

Brruuh would have seen none. Even Matter shifting to sit up, the siblings both tying up their hair created lines between work and relaxation.

And the aufenthaltsraum was comforting in the way Brruuh had always tried to make his office. It had plant life, soft blankets in YaPar orange and brown and YaBin greys. The sofas were fraying and patchworked together, but comfortable for both sitting and lounging and far larger than strictly necessary for such a small crew. The kitchen space was small, a glittering silver entity with chiller drawers and surprisingly deep cupboards. A hob, oven, kettle and coffee machine all with self-cleaning functions that he'd seen everyone use. It ended up being a perfect microcosm of how the crew worked together. Even if somebody left a mess, it rarely devolved into an argument, everyone accepting that messes happened and got forgotten, that people were called away for more important jobs from time to time. Nothing like when people left messes in Brruuh's old office kitchens.

"They said once the ship has passed muster, we can work inside the galaxy," Sebastian said.

"Not even the cluster?" Dimae asked.

Basti shook his head.

"It won't help anyway," Dimae muttered, huffing away his own question. "Nei harrushetti is going to want us to move their cargo when they could use a certified harrushetti vehicle instead."

"What then?" Matter asked. "We sit here and starve? Just wait for some random cognitivist to appear and hope they catch us on a good day? That's ridiculous."

"They're just trying to keep everyone safe," Basti placated. "And we're not going to starve, the Station is happy to provide for all our necessities while on board. You know that."

"Yum, Station canteen food designed primarily for obligate carnivores," Matter huffed. "And they don't care if we're safe. They're just following a stupid protocol. Protocol that means they're going to demand you find a new pilot. One who isn't like me."

"Matter…"

Matter shoved to their feet, coffee sloshing dangerously in the mug but not quite spilling over the edge. "Sorry, I'm not—I can't be in this conversation right now."

The conversation wrapped up quickly after their departure, the delicate balance of the crew meeting disrupted by their absence.

The crew of the Galactic Whale functioned in a very specific and particular way, not just because they were a small group, but by the interwoven layers to each of their relationships: Matter and Basti were siblings, though they hadn't grown up together, Dimae and Basti were married, Sauraxen and Basti were best friends from university, Matter and Sauraxen were somehow closer despite only having met through Basti's friendship with her. And, now, Brruuh was intertwined with Sauraxen by romantic relationship, and with Matter by the fact that they had brought him back from the brink of death. As if those social bonds weren't complex enough, the small number of crew led to a lot of crossover in duties: Matter was the pilot but functioned as a secondary engineer and security where necessary, Basti was the captain but he was also a backup medical officer, and despite being the medical officer Dimae also spent of a lot of time cooking for the entire crew.

Removing a single piece of this unit upset the balance.

Still, the other crew asked some questions. What would a harrushetti assessor want to see on a ship maintained by a wrexi? Because Sauraxen's perception of the world came though sensory feedback rather than sight, meaning nothing in engineering was labelled. A few questions from Basti to Brruuh about what the next stage of the process—a new cognitivist coming to reassess what he had tried and failed to assess—might look like. Not that Brruuh had ever run that kind of assessment himself.

When the conversation moved on to more casual items and Sauraxen shifted from cross-legged to perched on the balls of her feet on the sofa—position change proving that Brruuh was right in his assessment that the meeting was over—Brruuh excused himself to follow Matter.

They were in the pilot's console, the opposite end of the long living floor from the aufenthaltsraum, at the front of the ship with its huge domed window that normally displayed the wonder of space in all its glittering glory. Now it was just the sad grey walls of a Station's landing bay.

He elected to ignore the salt sting of tears in the air and the way Matter swiped a hand across their face. Standing at the edge of the room rather than stepping onto the narrow pathway to the main body of the pilots console. Giving Matter space where they perched in the tiltable and adjustable chair with its sidebar of buttons and dials Brruuh couldn't have begun to imagine the specific purpose of. "You okay?"

Matter shot him a grim smile. Such a human expression. No other species Brruuh had met would make such mockery of their own expression of happiness.

"Poor question," he admitted. "But I didn't know how else to open the conversation."

"What are you asking?"

"You hurt."

They shrugged a shoulder. "I always hurt."

"Emotionally hurt," he clarified.

Matter shrugged.

If this was a real cognitivism session, Brruuh would wait for Matter to say something more. He would never make suggestions, wouldn't risk putting words in Matter's mouth. But this wasn't a cognitivism session and Brruuh recognised a fear in himself that he wanted, rather selfishly, to find in someone else too. "You're afraid a harrushetti doctor won't clear you for duty?"

"It's not just that," Matter admitted. "It's the whole mess of having to be assessed at all. People constantly ask questions I don't want to answer: rude ones, reasonable ones. It doesn't matter. It becomes a *thing* that people want to know about." They put on a voice, "How did it happen? What does it mean? How long have you been like this? How do you manage?"

And if it wasn't questions, it was unsolicited comments on the state of the tragedy in question. *You lost your whole family? How old were you? Gosh, that's so sad! I could never.* Brruuh was uncomfortably familiar with that particular experience, even if his wasn't— hadn't been an injury.

"The not-questions are nei better," Matter continued. "Offering sympathy I didn't ask for. Sympathy I don't *want*. Telling me they wouldn't be able to live like me. As if this was a choice I made. As if suggesting that I should just stop."

Brruuh hummed noncommittally.

"As if they want me to disappear from their sight. Stars." They jerked away, turning their back to Brruuh, hand reaching up to their face again.

Tears. Human tears. Alien to Brruuh. Another piece of the mixed heritage that made up the confusing being before him. As a half-ouaeahhn, there was every chance Matter wouldn't have been landed with the emotions leaking from their eyes—ouaeahhn didn't do that. But Matter's half-human nature brought with it an odd variety of traits, their less holographic skin, their appetite, the way their presence read to the predator buried deep in Brruuh's instincts as a fellow threat, and the fact that they didn't bounce back the way other ouaeahhn had after the trauma they had shared with some of them.

"It's not like I chose this," Matter huffed into the landing bay outside the dome. The phantom ghost of their breath steaming against the clear protective bubble appearing in Brruuh's eye, even though the dome was too far for it to actually land. "I'm just doing what I can, you know?"

"I know," Brruuh breathed, afraid speaking too loudly would scare the words away. Matter was notably reticent to talk about any of this, Dimae—as chief medical officer—had brought that to Brruuh's attention more than once. Not outright asking him to try and work away at Matter's barriers, but pointing him in that general direction. Needing a greater understanding of their situation than Matter was willing to offer. And how could he blame them when it pressed against almost every area of their life? It got exhausting to talk about; at least Brruuh had been able to leave the place where everybody knew, at least Brruuh was able to disguise his symptoms, hide them from general view. Matter would be allowed no such recourse.

"Even Raxen asked." They sighed, fiddling with the coffee cup mostly abandoned on the little table attached to the pilot's chair. "And I get it, she's eaahla."

The translation module Brruuh had installed in his inbuilt translator murmured a rough translation: joy, interest, free-fall. What was the point of such direct word-centred translation when eaahla obviously meant such a specific thing here? But he would tuck it away and do the research later. And maybe he could get his claws on a proper IPA certified tele-empathy reader to add into the mix. Not that Matter was in the habit of leaving ouaeahhn language untranslated anyway.

"My best friend," they clarified after a thought, the words a little hesitant. Not a clean translation. Another concept like Ahthae—the family we. "She wants to know what to do to support me. But it's just so endless. Why can't I just…?"

"Just?"

"You never asked."

"Excuse me?"

Matter turned back to him, purple eyes intent and already starting to shine back his own silver grey colouring. "You never asked. After that initial cognitivism assessment where I gave you the Space Whale story, you just let it go. The only thing you pestered about was my ability to do my job, and you were far more focused on my unprofessional nature."

Brruuh shrugged, a very human gesture he'd

picked up from too many years working with them. "If I needed to know anything you would tell me. If you want my assistance, you'll tell me. Why would I need to know details? I'm not a medical doctor. Don't mistake, I'm happy for you to tell me as a friend or as a cognitivist, but it's only my business if you want it to be." Just like the situation with Brruuh's past, with his lost family. At least Matter wouldn't have to go into any medical assessment with the full knowledge that everyone involved recognised their markings as those of someone whose entire family, homestead, and community had been destroyed. "You're allowed an advocate," he said. "With the doctor."

Matter sighed. "Who would I ask? Basti, who gets choked with guilt ever time it comes up? As if he had any part in this. Sauraxen, who can't help but run as soon as she senses tension? Dimae, who doesn't even like me most of the time?"

"I'd do it."

Those eyes found his again and Brruuh found his ears flicking with embarrassment.

"I'll think about it."

Brruuh nodded and retreated from the pilot's console, back to his office. His safe professional space where he could take steps to help more than the immediate problem.

He pulled up the communications tab on his datapad and started tapping out a message to Vedran. He should start with an apology, right? Or would

Vedran even remember the cake incident? There had only been a little fire. And his eyebrows grew back in… After a while.

Ugh, why were social interactions so difficult?

Sauraxen

Pacing back and forth had the catwalk rattling under Sauraxen's feet. The grated metal dug into her scales, grounding her in the situation even as her senses rampaged to take in the cavernous cargo bay of Galactic Whale as the soundwaves bounced around. The lights were out, nothing trying to burn into her sensitive and all-but-useless eyes while her whole body absorbed those soundwaves to create a detailed understanding of every nook and cranny of the cargo bay. What point were eyes in the dark of the tunnels? When being able to feel every possible route to flee through tunnels without light was far more important? Instincts honed over years of evolution demanded she flee from the tension. As if running away could solve this particular problem.

In another reality she might have been able to knock like a human. In another reality she could have burst through the door. Been able to make her requests without needing to find words—Earth Common Eurean words at that—to explain what she needed. In another reality, she would be with other wrexi, who would know, would understand all the things she was struggling so hard to try and communicate. She wouldn't have to push past the boundary of human privacy to begin the conversation, wouldn't be daunted by the prospect of explaining the connections and reasoning. Wouldn't be worried she'd miscommunicate. Most wrexi learnt Earth Common Eurean as their IPA-Standard communication language, she was fluent beyond that learning, fluent enough that ECE came out in emotive moments as much as her parental-tongue of Wrexi.

The captain's cabin on Galactic Whale was set away from the living floor, offering a little extra privacy both ways. So a captain could escape their crew and so a crew could complain about their captain in peace. The door sat on the second level of the cargo bay, accessible only via the rattling catwalk and opposite the upper door to engineering. Sauraxen's domain. Even now the engines clicked and whirred in that comforting way they always did. Though only two engines were currently active: the home engine in charge of keeping lights running and air filtered, and the emergency engine to take over if the home engine died. The other two, designed for navigating out of atmospheres or through the vast cosmos of space sat silent. But they would function. Sauraxen had made sure of that.

She rapped her knuckles on the metal door, adding yet more sound and feedback to her senses.

Basti opened the door, hair in a blurry cloud around his head, sleep tousled. Loose trousers slung low on his hips and a sweatshirt in that comfy fuzzy-on-the-inside fabric Sauraxen liked to thief. She'd started that when they roomed together at uni, each on their Master's Degree course. A habit she'd carried into other close relationships: romantic and friendship based ones.

Some of his hair was tucked under the neckline, the usually expansive or tamed coils tugged close to his head. He'd obviously pulled the sweatshirt on to answer the door. Behind him, Dimae sat up in the huge captain's bed, large enough to fit an entire cuddle pile of wrexi. She tried to ignore him; he wasn't in line with the door, which meant he wasn't involving himself in the situation. That had been hard to learn about visual species. Their perception was so weird, and the rules about politeness even weirder. Had she remembered to put on clothes before coming down here? Another weird visual species rule she couldn't quite get used to no matter how long she lived off Pitzk.

"What's up?" Basti asked.

"I need to…" She searched for the words, wanted to show him the audio-message that had pulled her awake when everyone else on the ship was deep in their sleep cycles. But Basti wouldn't understand it, didn't speak the language the message had come through in.

It was rare to get messages from Pitzk. The atmosphere of the planet was inhospitable even to the creatures who lived there, packed with more sulphur than even the best filters could deal with for more than a short time. IPA standard messaging systems got stuck on each side of that sulphur, which was why the IPA had erected a signal tower. Of course, that tower had never been replaced since it was first installed, so all the messages had to be sent in an old fashioned format and someone had to take a datapad to the tower on a regular basis to send and receive off-planet post. Made worse, by the fact that every message was an audio file, which the IPA hadn't been exactly prepared to blast halfway across the universe. Every message got tossed into a queue when whoever got sent to the broadcast tower. All of that led to Sauraxen's decision to have messages originating from Pitzk come through with their own distinctive notification sound that played even through do not disturb settings.

Stuck as far away as Gnarresh-Fle in the

harrushetti galaxy, the squeak of a Pitzki notification had been exciting. A message from home, a comfort in times that seemed only to offer harsh edges and bright lights. A reply from her vava about all the dramatics of their Deep Space Travel assessment.

To his credit, Sebastian waited for her to find the words, rubbing the sleep out of his eyes—a tiredness habit for a human, not to be misinterpreted the wrexi way as exasperation.

"I need to go home," she managed.

"Home?"

"Pitzk."

"Is there a…?" He trailed off and shook his head, searching. "What?"

"I need to go to Pitzk. Now."

"Raxen, we're not allowed to leave the Station."

"I know but—"

"And Pitzk is… you need mandates and paperwork and—"

"My vava is sick." Not the comforting message she'd been hoping for when she opened it.

Basti froze in place. Normally humans shifted in all kinds of noisy ways, sometimes to the extent it would rebound of the world overwhelmingly. But now Sauraxen desperately sought more input, trying to figure out what he would do next, trying to ignore the way her instincts screamed that a predator stood before her frozen so he was ready to strike.

Basti let out a long slow breath. "Go wake the

others."

Dashing back up the gravity well to the living floor, she tried Matter first, knocking on the door of the quarters closest to the pilot's console. The one with something on it that, despite not being able to see it, nor having much of a tele-empathic score to speak of, still let out a feeling of home and comfort for Sauraxen. Matter appeared in minimal time, hair still hidden under the soft, dampening fabric they tended to wear at night. Sauraxen knew them well enough to recognise the lack of fastening on the jumpsuit meant they'd wriggled out of bed and straight into the nearest one.

She tried to ignore the sensation memory of knowing, oh so intimately, what it would feel like to slip those jumpsuit shoulders down Matter's arms and run her fingers all over their textured skin. Bared, because Matter wouldn't be wearing anything underneath.

But Sauraxen was in a relationship now. A closed one. No more casual sex with Matter. Not even to try and regulate her emotions in as stressful a situation as this. Wrexi did that, leaned on contact and connection to settle feelings before taking action. And Matter's casual, ouaeahhn, ideas about sex lent themselves to a friendship that allowed such contact. It had deepened the friendship Sauraxen and Matter shared beyond what Basti could offer, even if he had been Sauraxen's friend first. But Brruuh was harrushetti and harrushetti were monogamous—hyper-monogamous to the extent that most met, courted, and bonded with a single person over the course of their lifetime. Sauraxen's relationships had been more fluid, some monogamous, some polyamorous, some open, some closed. It was easier for her to meet Brruuh at monogamy than ask him to expand his instinctive and culturally important nature. Even if it didn't feel like that right now in the face of bad news and a comforting friend.

"Coffee," Matter insisted, voice rough. "We can fix it after coffee."

How did they know something needed fixing?

"Empath," Matter called over their shoulder as she started into the aufenthaltsraum, pulling the fabric off their head to let all that hair tumble down their back.

By the time Sauraxen had woken Brruuh from the quarters across the hall from his office and they'd all gathered in the communal kitchen space, Matter had finished making drinks.

"My vava," Sauraxen explained.

"What's a vava?" Dimae interrupted. The only member of the crew who had taken the time to dress properly—unless one counted Sauraxen and Matter each slipping into something that looked professional from the outside—wrapped in a criss-cross cardigan that was a little more casual than his usual medical-wear.

"Raising parent," Matter answered, knocking back

pain killer tablets with too-hot coffee that made them hiss steam out of their mouth.

"Xe is sick," Sauraxen continued. "I just got the message. I need to—" She started to pace back and forth in front of the dining table, trying to mitigate the need to run. "I need to be with— I need to get back to Pitzk before it's too late."

"And you can't catch a shuttle?" Dimae asked.

Basti nudged him.

"Nei, I'm not being harsh," Dimae protested. "We're mandated to stay. Surely a shuttle would…" He trailed off as Sauraxen shook her head.

"People rarely travel to Pitzk because of how inhospitable it is. There's not much there either. I love my home planet but it's not what the IPA terms valuable. Wrexi are about all that exist there… Wrexi and mushrooms."

"Brruuh," Basti asked, "Do you know any IPA regulations that can get us there?"

"What is your vava unwell with?" Brruuh asked, a soft rumble underneath the words. He pressed hands against his pyjamas—a long tunic-top with slits up the sides for ease of movement worn over loose trousers. When he didn't find what he was looking for, he reached across the dining table to grab Sebastian's discarded datapad. That thing seemed to live somewhere in the aufenthaltsraum.

"It's a wrexi disease," Sauraxen explained. "If I had to translate it…" She took a deep breath, trying to find words and fighting against the image of other wrexi she had seen suffering this. The way the breath rattled in their chests. The way their movement slowed and shifted. The way they passed over food, unable to eat, unable to…

Arms snaked around her waist, a chin pressing gently into the top of her head. Pizza pockets and coffee: Matter. They rubbed their chin against her hair, the shift a comfort more like what Brruuh would offer.

"Wasting," Sauraxen said finally, tucking closer to Matter.

"We could apply for medical emergency dispensation," Brruuh suggested. The rumble of his secondary vocal cords changed tone. "Or grief leave if…"

"I've never known anyone recover from this," Sauraxen admitted.

"That paperwork will take weeks," Dimae argued, "Especially from here." He glanced at Sauraxen, head turning, ears flicking. "Won't it be too late by then?"

"Ja," Brruuh shrugged. "But we can always fill out the paperwork and travel under the assumption of permission."

"What?"

"Assumption of permission. It's a thing. Unofficially. You put in the paperwork request, assume permission will be granted, and most regulatory bodies let it slide. Even if permission is refused after the fact. Even if there is trouble, it is usually less. We all know how long the IPA takes to respond to paperwork." Brruuh shrugged. "It has risks, on occasion the repercussions are far greater. If you get a real rule-follower, there's trouble. There are consequences. But…"

Matter kissed the top of Sauraxen's head and grabbed their coffee from the table. "I'll get us set off then."

Matter

During their time docked at Gnarresh-Fle Inter-Planetary Alliance Station, Sauraxen and Matter had both been hard at work getting the ship fixed up. Matter's main focus had been inside their own domain of the pilot's console. The poor thing had been through the wringer during their official Deep Space Travel Assessment. At least Basti hadn't had to pay for the damage outright. Insurance. Jonesy had insisted on it so strictly that he'd taken out a secondary policy labelling himself as 'investor'. That had been an awkwardly avoided conversation, the voicemail recording playing so loudly the entire ship heard it. Matter wouldn't have been surprised if the entire Station had.

Basti sending a 'we're okay' text afterward was… bold. And exactly the kind of action Matter took when it came to their shared parent. Especially when he was loud like that.

The other crew had spent most of the time on Gnarresh-Fle in the medi-centre, with the brief exception of Basti trying to get a meeting with a bureaucrat, each day less of a limp to his step on his broken hip. Matter hadn't bothered with it at all. What was the point? It was all part of the same problem and they certainly didn't want to invite new doctors to puzzle over them. They didn't need that hover chair Basti had tried to secret away with the replacement shuttle, so everything was fine. Meaningful contact would solve what it could and painkillers would soften the rest. The fact that meaningful contact was proving hard to find was neither here nor there. They'd figure it out. They always did.

Shaking off the melancholy thoughts, Matter laid their fingers over the controls, sending the engines humming to life. A voice blasted through inter-ship comms. Stars, how had they still not fixed the volume on that thing?

"Galactic Whale, please turn off your engines, you are not cleared for departure."

Matter ignored it, keeping their eyes pinned to the landing bay doors: humongous sliding metal that split into four pieces to best allow ships to fit through. The orange and green hashed edges had been battered over the years, paint peeling to allow the grey metal beneath to peek through.

To their side, another ship's atmospheric thrusters lit that delicate blue that most IPA thrusters did. Basti compared it to the flame of a Bunsen burner, but Matter thought it looked more like the tail of a comet.

"Galactic Whale," the voice came again, battering at Matter's ears. "Scope-3 is cleared for liftoff, please turn your engines off to allow them clear exit."

Sorry Scope-3, nei can do.

The little boxy craft lifted off the docking bay floor, hovering awkwardly like a dragonfly over a pond, as if struggling to maintain altitude. It corrected and headed for the opening doors. The peek of the glittering void through the orange and green caution bars.

Matter's heart thumped against their chest. A thrumming bassline to the event itself, like an action vid in progress with music overlaid. As Scope-3 exited the space, the atmospheric bubble shield shone and rippled in its wake. Matter's hands flew over the controls, and Galactic Whale burst out into the void, catching only a little on the closing docking bay doors as they did so.

Station Control called out, blaring over the ship comms, but Matter ignored it.

Out in the void again, controls under their hands,

Matter reclined in the chair. The situation was bad. Objectively speaking, they were doing illegal stuff and Sauraxen might lose her only relevant parent. But something light and joyous bubbled in Matter's chest as they looked up into all those stars. All those possibilities shining in front of them.

They had almost expected fear. After their last official grounding, getting back in the pilot's chair had brought a discomfort that rose in them like acid reflux, a burning anxiety that kept them checking and double checking their instruments and sides and all the potentials the void offered for threats. Being towed to Gnarresh-Fle had been tough too, had brought that same discomfort. The instant disconnect of being so visibly out of control, as a tractor beam buzzed around the edge of the ship, so different to the hum of the engines. Matter expected it would linger.

They should have known better. In the aftermath of the events in Clickclick, with their whole Ahthae hurting and dying from illegal weapons, Matter had done some of the best piloting of their entire life. After what had felt like forever piloting through a disgustingly cluttered galaxy, after Basti had been tricked and imprisoned and blackmailed, Matter had managed what nobody but an experienced ouaeahhn pilot could have hoped for. Could have dreamed of. And, honestly, even then, maybe nobody else including another ouaeahhn could have done it. Maybe it could only have been Matter who noticed that comet tail sparkling the same grey as Brruuh's' eyes, the front of it glowing the yellow of the delicate spots on Sauraxen's mushrooms. And maybe nobody else would have been reckless enough to use atmospheric thrusters to shove themself in front of a comet at all.

And it had meant Matter did the one thing they always wanted to manage: they made sure people didn't suffer the same fate they had. The crew were alive, mostly unharmed, and nobody had had to watch anyone else wither and die. Matter's piloting had made sure they stayed that way. And now they had a job to do for Sauraxen.

Sauraxen, the friend who had been as steady and constant in Matter's life as the very stars above them. Her easy wrexi smiles and peeping laugh that brought a level of ease to Matter's woes. Sauraxen, who knew how to take care of them on bad days. Who never asked too much. Who always seemed to see when Matter needed something. She was their security, their comfort, their home.

They wouldn't fail her.

Travel
Day 1

Dimae

The rap of knuckles on the door of Medi-Bay pulled Dimae away from his task. He should have heard someone coming, should have smelled them, noticed before they had to announce themself by knocking. But he hadn't. Just like he hadn't actually been focusing on the task.

How long would these frustrating continuing symptoms last? How long until he could escape the thoughts and memories of almost dying and get back to who he was meant to be? How long until he felt normal again?

With a shaky breath, he closed the cupboard door and pushed to his feet to greet Matter where they stood in the open door of medi-bay. They looked more like themself than they had at the recent meetings, hair back in its usual pair of buns on top of their head, skin glittering in the light only partially obscured by their jumpsuit. "What do you need?" he asked. "Are you in pain?"

"What a question," Matter joked.

Dimae huffed, an acknowledgement of their intended humour, even if he didn't actually find the humour in it. He was trying to be more patient with Matter's oddities. Trying to be more accepting of the family he had found himself in, no matter how much it went against his culture.

Matter's face shifted, eyes sliding to one side: avoidance. Basti pulled the exact same expression. "I know I'm not medically certified or anything and I'm nei cognitivist and I probably don't rank on your list of people to talk to about this but…"

"But?"

"With Basti being your husband—Bond Mate. And Brruuh also being in recovery and therefore an active patient of yours. I thought you might benefit from the knowledge that someone else is here if you wanted to… talk?"

"I'm fine," Dimae tried not to snap, the beginnings of a growl humming under his words.

"Great," Matter grinned. "Glad to hear it. And if that ceases to be the official line you're sticking to, I'm here. You claimed me back, you said you were honoured to be part of my Ahthae, this is part of the deal."

Dimae scrunched his nose but there was fondness to it. Matter was right. By both human and ouaeahhn standards, they were family, even if that still seemed so alien to him. Half-siblings didn't exist on Harrush—couldn't with the hyper-monogamy leading to death if a partner left by any means: choice, happenstance, or mortality. It had been difficult to fit Matter into his view of families, so he hadn't. He hadn't needed to until they started working together. Only seeing a person when you both made it back for terraforming day at the same time didn't require much by way of allowances.

"I get not wanting to talk about it," Matter said quietly. "Fucks knows I don't like talking about stuff. But if you need it, need someone to complain to without it being taken further, someone to reassure you that it won't say this bad forever, or wallow with you for a while, I'm your choice. Or an option—that translates better in ouaeahhn: Ahhmm."

"Was that all?" Dimae asked.

Matter nodded but didn't turn to leave.

"What else?" Dimae couldn't help but smile.

"I'm running low on pain meds. I ordered some on Gnarresh-Fle but they didn't come in before we left."

Dimae grabbed a box from his cupboard. With only brief contemplation he tossed it to them. What would be the point in making them keep returning for more? Allowing Dimae to be more in charge of a condition Matter managed perfectly well alone? Dimae had never really understood it before, had never been in a position of… fear for his capabilities. Or fear that others would believe him less capable because of the trauma his body sustained. He'd always thought signing people off for disability was helpful, that it was the best choice. And certainly there were appropriate times. But had he ignored people's wants and made these executive judgements that trapped people down the way he was so desperate not to have done to him? Had he been too quick to do it? Locked someone like Matter or himself out of the thing that made them shine?

Matter shook the box at him in a thanks before disappearing back into the cargo bay. Dimae turned back to his supplies, trying not to linger on the idea that he had ruined someone's life when he was only ever trying to help. His whole job was supposed to be helping people feel better.

He sighed again, flicking over what little he'd recorded of their supplies and removing a box of the good painkillers. There was no choice here, they needed to make a stop. Needed supplies he didn't have. Especially if they were to land on Pitzk.

His ears pitched down toward his head. He didn't

want to ask Sauraxen for extras days, not when his inevitable practicality always came across too harsh to the others. He didn't want to risk her losing her last chance to spend time with her vava. But he had a duty of care to the whole crew, not just her.

Would he make the same choice if it was Jonesy? If he knew the person dying? If it was Basti's person? Would he still prioritise the needs of the rest of the crew?

Sebastian

Basti toyed with the communications tab on his wristband, flicking it open and closed. Open and closed. Open, scroll down, and closed. Occasionally his fingers lingered over the call button but he hadn't quite managed to press it.

Sauraxen nearly losing her vava made him want to call. But Basti hadn't spoken to his mama in years now. Not since he told her his plans to buy his own ship. It had taken a long time after that to get the money together at all, and she had never once reached out or apologised for the things she had said. She hadn't even had the decency to pretend she didn't say them. Basti wouldn't even go home if he knew she was going to be there. She always ended up going into detail about how she thought his choices were bad ones and why. She'd even started trying to pull Dimae onto her side.

He rubbed his face. How could he hope to help Sauraxen through this if he purposefully hadn't spoken to one of his parents in more years than he wanted to count? When she hadn't called for his fortieth birthday, that had been the end for their relationship, but now… How could he hope to offer comfort to his friend in a situation like this? And as a captain…?

"What'cha doing?" Matter asked, sweeping into the room with a box full of rattling tablets that they tossed carelessly onto the table next to Basti. It didn't even have a prescription tab on it.

"Thinking about calling mama."

"Eek. Coffee?"

Basti let out a breath of relief. "Always."

Matter set about making drinks, the unmistakable scent of chocolate mixing with the coffee.

"You think it's serious enough for mochas?" he couldn't help but whine.

"When was the last time you spoke to her?"

Basti leaned back in the chair and rubbed his face. Had it been a birthday? Or terraforming day when he didn't know she was going to be on planet? Either way she had berated his life choices again. She told him aiming for his own ship was foolish and she would be happy to support him going for captaincy on an IPA-run vessel. She wanted to know why he was so intent on a 'low brow task' like cargo running instead of something 'more valuable' like exploration or research. She wanted to know how Dimae felt about Basti 'yanking him away from the cutting edge of medicine' in order to 'gallivant about the galaxy like a pair of ruffians'. As if Basti wouldn't have discussed that with the man he intended to spend the rest of his life with. But he could hardly expect his parents to understanding wanting to spend time with their partner, since neither of them was willing to sacrifice wants to spend time together.

She hadn't wanted answers anyway. It didn't matter to her what appealed about cargo running. That people needed cargo. That the entire farm his father ran relied on cargo runners to keep going. And apparently it mattered equally little that his sister, Peggy, was trying to go into singing when that was an even less reliable career choice.

"I'm not going to do it," he admitted. "Call her."

"Oh?"

"What would I say? Hi mama, nei my business isn't running well, I'm actually illegally moving to a planet you need a license to land on. Nei I don't have that licence either."

"I guess that's why you didn't think to call her for permission either."

"What?"

"Isn't she some IPA high up?"

"I don't even know anymore. It's been, what? How old am I now?"

"Forty-f—"

"Nei! Don't start!"

Matter tossed their head back in a laugh. "You asked!"

"At least papa has the decency to say 'I don't get it but if it's what you want'."

"I literally cannot imagine those words coming out of Jonesy's mouth."

Basti blew out a breath. Matter hadn't met their shared father until into their adulthood and there was always something just a little too awkward about their interactions. Like he couldn't get past the way Matter's alien-ness glittered across their face. Or maybe he just wanted to make up for years of lost parenting but going too hard on an adult who already had an established sense of self and want. "Parents are hard."

"For sure," Matter agreed, shifting into the chair opposite him, face twisting a little with the pain of the movement.

"You okay?"

Matter shot him a flat look and slid his mocha toward him.

He stared into the mug, watching the light reflecting off the liquid inside. "Do you have parents on Ouaeahhn?"

"It's complicated."

"Right…" Basti blew on the liquid in the mug. Complicated, also known as, 'I don't want to talk about it'. There had been a lot of those recently.

"It's a tele-empathic planet, Basti, you can converse with a tree, or an animal, or the ground you walk on—to an extent. It's really hard to explain to a null species. But at its core, the whole planet raises saplings and you can only make them through choice but any number of people can be involved in the choice."

Basti could feel his face twist trying to figure out how that worked.

"Told you you wouldn't get it." They dug an almost finished strip of painkillers out of a pocket. Basti said nothing about the box discarded on the table as Matter popped two tablets and chased them with mocha. "If this is all because Sauraxen is struggling with her own parent situation, she's not going to hold your situation against you. Your personal parental tensions have nei bearing on her. That's not how she works."

"I know…"

"But?"

"I guess it's not about her. It's not about mama either."

Matter nodded, trailing their fingers over the rim of the mug. "It's about Dimae."

"What? How did you get there?"

They shrugged a shoulder. "Fear of loss. The person you're most afraid of losing. The person who understands you best in the whole world. For someone like you, it's him. And with everything that just happened…"

"What if I'm not enough? What if he gets hurt again and I'm not enough to save him?"

Matter took his hands, gripping tight to his fingers. "You are always enough, Basti. Especially for him. It just might take a little longer than you think."

"You two saved Brruuh with barely any connection and I couldn't—" His breath hitched.

"Sauraxen and I build connection fast and deep. We go from acquaintance to friend to apparently-lover within weeks or months—you know they're together too, right?—And Brruuh still has a level of kitten about him that Dimae is long away from. Not to mention any tele-empathic bonds. The situation was different. You can't hold our success up as your failure. Not if you want to keep going."

"What do you mean?"

"Anlani." They sighed out the ouaeahhn word, eyebrows twitching as they tried to build a translation. "The false feeling of loss will break you. It will take you from the stars until everything is dark. You have stars still, he's still here. He's mostly fine. Celebrate that, don't wish him away with your pessimism."

"Is that how you live with it?"

"With what?"

"Your pain?"

Matter's grip turned cold in his hands. They swallowed, extracting their hands and cupping the mug instead.

"You look at the stars you still have," Basti tried to clarify, knowing it would be as pointless as explaining cargo running to mama. He'd fucked up. Offered hurt instead of commiseration.

"I should get back to flying."

"You know," Basti muttered to himself, slouching over his coffee. "You're a real Jonesy sometimes, Sebastian."

Brruuh

Brruuh had successfully rearranged his entire office. Twice. Originally the space had been one of the crew quarters aboard Galactic Whale, one of eight matching spaces on the living floor—separated from the captain's quarters over the cargo bay—each with its own door, bed, desk, and wardrobe. This one had been lacking important pieces that would have allowed it to function and, since Galactic Whale had fewer than eight non-captain crew, Brruuh had claimed the space as an office while he was running the Deep Space Travel assessment.

There wasn't much by way of rearranging he could actually do with the two large, comfy chairs he had wrangled in here in the first place. But Brruuh had whittled away several hours with the ship humming quietly beneath his feet moving and moving back the assorted pieces of comfort he had placed in the space. Hiding wasn't a word he'd like to use for what he was doing, but it might be accurate despite his feelings about it.

With the damage the ship sustained in the last few days of that DST assessment, Brruuh had been surprised to find the repairs completed within such a short timeframe. Even with Sauraxen's reputed expertise, Brruuh couldn't truly engage with the idea that the rubbled thing towed to Gnarresh-Fle from Harrush was now, in fact, serviceable. The quiet buzz accompanying its movements twitching in his sensitive ears and between his paw pads was the only remaining evidence of the damage. Now a life affirming sensation, as if the ship itself was as alive as the crew within it.

Going to Pitzk was difficult. Brruuh had lost his entire family and clan, which meant starting a relationship with Sauraxen didn't risk having to introduce her to anyone important. He had never considered Sauraxen having a family, especially after she'd explained how wrexi families worked. Wrexi came together to create eggs, which hatched in their own time, letting a tiny baby wrexi start wandering and crying out for support, which a vava—a raising parent—would hear and instinctively come to gather and support them to adulthood. All of which made Brruuh think that there was nobody to be introduced to. To be going now, at such a difficult time...

The warring nature of wanting to appeal to a parent whose culture he barely knew, the inescapable gut-deep memory of losing family was more than Brruuh knew how to deal with, even with all his extensive understanding of the cognitive processes and managing emotion. Maybe he should reach out to a trusted colleague about this. But would that put their entire mission at risk? He could ask Vedran, if Vedran ever got back to him.

Sauraxen popping through the door yanked him thoroughly out of his rumination. It was still so breath-taking to remember this lizardoid who glittered like the heart of his home planet was real and had chosen him. So easy to slip into thoughts of sliding the thin strapped playsuit off her shoulders and burying his nose and mouth against her neck to take in her full scent. Letting her hair wrap around him like tentacles.

He shook himself out of his reverie.

"Where have you been?" she asked.

Brruuh gestured sweepingly to the room around

him. Did it even look different?

"Let me rephrase, why are you hiding here?"

Brruuh rubbed his ear, a kittenish self-soothe he had used to be more self-conscious about. He wanted to lie, to claim he hadn't been hiding at all. "Introductions are important on Harrush."

"Oh?"

"Ja. I've told you some of our courting rituals."

"Cloak-bearer and dancer," Sauraxen confirmed.

Brruuh's nose twitched in amusement. Such a simplified way of explaining the intricate interaction where one partner would request the other bear their cloak to allow them to prove prowess in a dance that had once been combat. An invitation to be looked after and protected, to become a homesteader, kept warm and safe and offered the duty to maintain a stable, dry life. Still, it got the point across, she remembered. "After that, after the courting has been accepted and confirmed, we introduce our paramour to our family. The bonding ceremony is the formal induction into the family, but we often do introductions before that. If the family doesn't approve..." He took a breath. "The courting ends."

That was that. It depended entirely on the riarch, the head of the household. If the riarch—in Brruuh's case his grandfather, a strict man, stripes ingrained so deeply down his face that they looked more like scars—didn't approve, with a single flick of an ear they could turn out a paramour. It had happened to

Brruuh's cousin once, while Brruuh was still too young to really know what a relationship was. Ahou had brought home a dancer; Brruuh had seen them in the central square under the light of the harrushti star and had marvelled at the parts where claws had clashed, sending sparks skittering across the floor. Then Ahou brought them home and grandfather had flared his nostrils, right ear flicking back, and Ahou had escorted the dancer out.

Brruuh hadn't really understood it at the time. Too young. Too excited about special food. He'd ended up bored and playing with the tablecloth anyway as arguments raged over his head. And that was his entire lived experience with harrushetti courting rituals. Everything else he had learnt through research.

"That's not really a thing on Pitzk," Sauraxen said.

"You've told me relationships as I know them don't exist there either."

Before they had begun anything, when Sauraxen was trying to reassure him that a recent breakup was no reason to worry about her making rash or regrettable decisions about joining a Deep Space Crew. She had been explaining how complex wrexi relationships could be, how they took things case by case, and that monogamy had been a new concept when she left her home planet.

They'd got into it further when Brruuh had been stumbling over his attempts to declare his feelings. It would have been far easier if he could have handed over a cloak, but Sauraxen wouldn't have had a hope of knowing what that meant. She'd explained that wrexi-wrexi relationships—or wrexi-wrexi-wrexi and more relationships—consisted mostly of shared couplings, but long term wasn't expected. Since then, they'd had more theoretical discussions about whether monogamy was more inclined in cultures that raised the children they made, where it wasn't in more community-focused raising.

"That's... true." She let out of peep of wrexi language. "My vava will love you, try not to worry about it."

"You talk as if there are nei other options."

She slipped her arms around him. "There aren't. Vava will love you because I do. We don't have relationships on Pitzk, so xe might not understand, but xe will love you because I chose you. All that harrushetti pressure you're imagining, it doesn't exist on Pitzk either."

Brruuh nuzzled into her neck. The overture of engine oil and warmed metal filling his nose, carried by that undercurrent that was specifically Sauraxen. "I just want to make the right impression."

"You know that hum thing you do?"

Brruuh let out a soft almost-purr.

"Ja, that. That's comforting and alerting. It announces your presence so you don't disappear into stillness like a horrifying predator. If you can do that you'll set everyone, especially vava, at ease."

"Horrifying predator?" Brruuh asked.

"Ja."

As if he wasn't scared before.

Travel
Day 2

Sauraxen

Brruuh had started spending at least some of the night cycle in Sauraxen's room. As a member of a species who slept in short bursts, he rarely both started and ended a night there, disappearing part way through or requesting entry later on, all around what he called 'restful activities' like botany or fibre crafts. He did it often enough now that she'd pulled together a dim lamp for him out of some pieces from her junk drawer. There were certainly things that needed her attention on the ship, things that were more urgent or more important, or more useful than a little lamp so her boyfriend stopped bashing his legs every time he came into her room. But Sauraxen was the one who could make that decision.

He'd also started to leave some items in the room: some clothes, some pyjamas, one of his blankets, and a small piece he had knitted or crocheted himself, which felt a lot like the shape of a mushroom.

It was one of those nights—one of those times Brruuh knocked gently, the sound now familiar enough that she knew it was him without any further input. He always waited for the invitation, but at least now he recognised the Wrexi version so she didn't have to find Earth Common Eurean from the depths of sleep when Wrexi came out first.

He slid the door closed behind him and Sauraxen flicked on the new lamp. Dim enough to only create a soft aura around her eyes the way Pitzki mushrooms did. Dimmer than any of the standard lights on Galactic Whale, which were themselves dimmer than most IPA standard lights. Brruuh let out an explosive purr. "You made this for me?"

"Of course. I wanted to make you comfortable."

He clambered into the bed with her and nuzzled close. The bed had shifted to accommodate Brruuh too. She had originally set up a secluded sleeping area under the desk, only using the official bed for couplings, but when Brruuh started staying she wanted it to be easier to share. A nice new hoop attached to the ceiling let blankets cascade around the sleeping area now big enough for two, enough to replicate a cavern without pinning Brruuh in. Not that she needed so much cavern-mimicking when Brruuh was in here with her. She never had when sleeping with a paramour—or with Matter.

Stop thinking about Matter.

"What's wrong?" Brruuh asked, voice soft the way it always seemed to be at night.

Sauraxen tried not to pull her hair tightly to herself with a grimace. "I was just thinking—comparing."

"That's new for me," Brruuh admitted on a sigh, fingers trailing along her scales. "I never considered whether a partner would compare me to an ex—never expected to find a partner, let alone one who had exes to consider."

"You never expected to find a partner?" As far as Sauraxen understood it, staying single on Harrush was pretty rare. As a hyper-monogamous species who could literally die of heartbreak if rejected or widowed, they valued romance and partnership as a truly special thing that everyone deserved and should aim for.

"My development was… altered. Most harrushetti find me strange."

Right. Because of the flood and the destruction of his home. Which Sauraxen only knew about because a random doctor had blabbed the whole thing to her and Matter in a pessimistic monologue about not expecting Brruuh to survive.

"I find you strange too," she teased.

Brruuh chuckled lowly.

"But I like it." She nuzzled into his chest, letting his heart beat softly against her scales. "I was thinking about the fact that you're comforting to have around, and how Matter is similarly comforting."

"You used to… couple with Matter?"

Warm smooth skin, layered with patterns and markings under her touch. Their wet mouth and tongue. Experience leading to new discoveries. The closeness of friendship allowing for ease of communication: I like that, and don't do that again, and can I try that on you. All so different from being with Brruuh, his short fur insulating him, barring his body temperature from Sauraxen, his dry barbed tongue all kinds of texture on its own. Caution built on the newness of their relationship, more reassurance with requests as Brruuh discovered what he liked at all alongside learning what Sauraxen knew of her own preferences.

"Casually," Sauraxen clarified. She'd never formed a bond outside friendship with Matter. It was just that friendship with Matter could include sex, same as friendships on Pitzk could.

"You're so alien."

"I literally am an alien to you," Sauraxen confirmed, trying not to laugh. Something about this felt serious, even if they were both speaking in light and casual tones.

Brruuh levered a hand under his head, chest shifting against Sauraxen but not dislodging her. "Matter is comforting," he breathed. "They're pleasant to be around."

"I'm glad you think so. They're my best friend. We only…" She pressed her face to his side, fighting the urge to laugh again at the continuing use of her poorly chosen word. "Coupled for comfort and friendship. It's not…" she couldn't say love, she did love Matter. It was just a different sort than what she shared with Brruuh. "Don't be jealous."

"I don't think I am. Which is… unexpected."

Sauraxen slid up him to press her mouth to his. In response, Brruuh's hands slipped to more purposeful action than the casual trails he had been tracing.

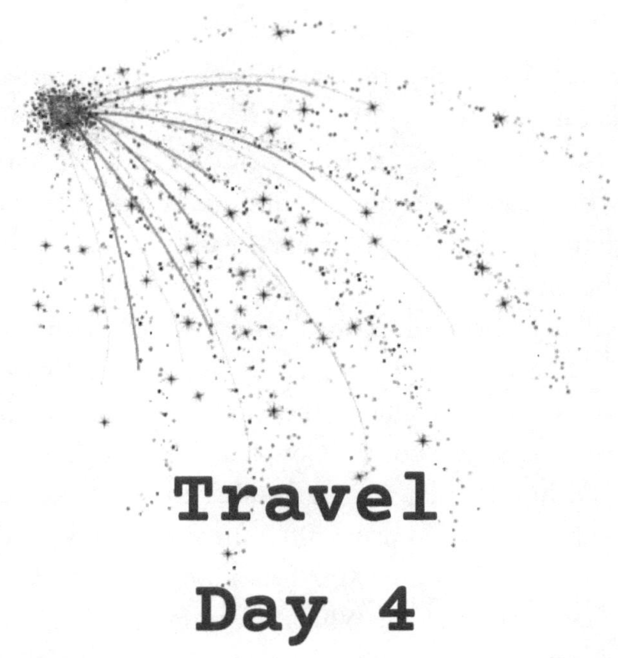

Travel
Day 4

Sebastian

Refuelling stops usually ended up placed on moons or miniature space stations. Moons were, by and large, the more pleasant of the two. Their gravity cycle was a little more stable, a little less likely to interfere with ship controls or damage people when they stepped out. Not that anyone else on the crew could manage this particular level of gravity. Heavy enough to obscure all sensory input for Sauraxen, heavy enough to mess with harrushetti balance. Matter might have been able to, but Matter wasn't available, so Basti had come out by himself.

The space was pretty barren. Not one of those stops with a bustling culture thriving within. This one had no permanent habitants, lending it a hollow, haunted air that Basti didn't much appreciate. A crate stacker sat close to the docking pad, along with some refuel pistons and battery charging ports, all designed to be used on an honour system. A little further away from the landing zone, a tower of IPA-grey building stretched: a hostel for anyone who needed to stay over. Basti had done it once. He'd been heading from one cluster to another to join a ship. The tiny shuttle he'd been shoved into allowed only one pit stop at a refuelling station just like this one. The bedrooms in those hostels were utterly dehumanising—depersonising?—bedding, towels and other necessities went through an electronic cleaning and folding system, but guests had to put them on and take them off the beds for themselves. Not fun when you'd spent the last two days in a cramped shuttle hurtling through space and trying not to barf on yourself and when all you could think of was flopping into a soft bed and sleeping stretched out for a change. Then maybe a shower once sleep was over with.

Most of the food available at the one Basti had stayed in was rehydratable and tasted of exactly nothing. Worse still coffee was rare: most stimulants were in places like these, since they could be dangerous for certain aliens. Most commonly you could find flavoured sugar powder to put in water, but human taste buds only really picked up the sugar part of that, not so much the flavour portion. At least in Basti's experience. Except for that one that tasted like salt for some reason.

On this moon, in an otherwise uninhabited galaxy somewhere between Harrush and Pitzk, there was a crate in the pickup zone with Basti's ship registration number printed on the side in Romanised lettering—a risk they had needed to take since they objectively needed these supplies. But it didn't look like there was any kind of IPA sting operation waiting for them here.

In less intense gravity, Basti would have been able to lift the crate alone, as it was… Between the crate being just a little longer than his arm span and the gravity pressing on his shoulders like a weighted vest, it wasn't looking promising. "I do not want to ask Matter to come do this," he muttered to himself, attempting once again to heft the crate. "What did we even order?"

"Need a hand?" a smooth voice asked, lightly accented with something Basti recognised but couldn't place.

"Ja, that would be great," Basti agreed readily.

The other side of the crate raised, allowing Basti to

grip his half.

"It's just that Ribbit over there," Basti said, using the slang term for his R1bb1t style vessel, since they still hadn't engraved the name on the side yet. It wasn't like there were a plethora of other ships here, let alone ones with boarding planks extended, light spilling down to glow beneath the ship itself. Just his stupid and wonderful bobbly frog-like thing.

The boarding plank rattled and clanked at the pair treaded their way up it. He really needed to get that fixed. As soon as they stepped into the ship's shield barrier, the weight tugging Basti down lifted. His temporary companion let out a little 'ooft' at the change, crate almost unbalancing between them.

Once the crate was in the cargo bay, the looming space seeming to shrink the crate by comparison, Basti looked over to thank the helpful stranger and found himself frozen because the person across the crate from him was ouaeahhn.

It wasn't that ouaeahhn were rare—they were founding members of the IPA, and Basti had met plenty over the years. It wasn't even that they were particularly recognisable, though with that holographic skin and hair that shimmered to reflect their surroundings like a mirror, they were. It wasn't even that finding a single ouaeahhn travelling alone was unusual, though since they needed meaningful contact to survive and having no companion made that a lot more challenging, it was. No, it was noticing how little Matter had started to shine by comparison.

The ouaeahhn took a cautious step back toward the boarding plank.

"Sorry," Basti blurted. "Didn't mean to get struck like that, just haven't seen another ouaeahhn in a while."

"Another?"

"My pilot, Matter, is ouaeahhn too."

"Your pilot's name is 'movement and'?"

"What? Oh, no, their full name is Ee-matter-ah-ni." He sounded it out, still a struggle even after all these years.

"Ymmattrahni?" Pronounced with that perfect fluency of a person familiar with the language, but something felt off, an emotion Basti couldn't name seeming to accompany what was normally a comforting thing to hear.

"Ja," Basti confirmed despite the feeling, trying not to get distracted by how this literal stranger did a better job with Matter's name than he could. How alienating would it be to constantly have to alter your name just so people could pronounce it? Picking out the part of it that appeared in IPA easy-linguistics and engineers-lang because that would allow almost everyone to figure something mostly right.

"I'm Hnan."

"Hn-Aan?"

The ouaeahhn smiled. "Close enough."

"I'm Sebastian."

"Sebastian?" It came out more like Seba-shun, but Basti decided not to comment on that considering his sounding out of Matter's name. "Do you take passengers?"

"We're a cargo runner," Basti started, as if they were legally transporting anything right now. "But we have some spare beds, where are you headed?"

"I'm Ma-se. I travel."

"Come up to the living floor and I'll introduce you to the crew and maybe pick out where you want to be dropped off."

Hnan followed Basti up the gravity lift. Before Basti could lead him into the aufenthaltsraum, Hnan stopped in his tracks. Basti opened his mouth to ask but Hnan was already moving toward Matter's quarters. They hadn't appeared out of them yet today, something most of the crew were well-practised in ignoring. They'd come out when they wanted to. When they were ready.

"Ymmattrahni," Hnan breathed, trailing fingers over the sign on their door, Ouaeahhn letters overlaid by Romanised ones. "They're broken."

"Excuse me?" Basti snapped, ready to dump the ouaeahhn right back out onto the moon.

"Something is wrong with them. I can feel it." He slid the door open without knocking, leaving Basti in the hallway alone and stumped. Should he follow? Follow the plan and set the autopilot going? Matter could handle themself, right?

Matter

It would be nice if big pain days could, at the very least, place themselves at more convenient times. Ugh, most people probably didn't have thoughts like that. Most people probably would have hoped for no big pain days at all. But Matter was well-past understanding what pain-free felt like. To the extent that 'the normal amount' as an answer got the stern looks from medical sorts.

Unfortunately, pain days didn't much care what your plans were, they didn't care if you were landing for the first time since your ship had been damaged and repaired, they didn't care that you might need a fanciful getaway from IPA ships if your best friend was going to make it back home before her vava died, and they didn't care if you were supposed to be helping Basti load cargo.

Matter had woken up with it. The pain. Had known immediately that there was no point even trying to make it to the aufenthaltsraum. Because if they tried to get out of the bed, their limbs would make like jelly and let them slide into a pile on the floor. Beds were, generally, more comfortable than the floor. The looming presence of that hover chair rankled hardest on days like this. Days where it would be useful if only Matter's stupid pride didn't get in the way.

Let the autopilot hold out.

Matter dragged their blanket closer around them, hugging the space whale Brruuh had made for their birthday closer to their chest. They could reach for painkillers, but would it help? Would it make a dent? Or would it just eat through their already short supply?

They closed their eyes and tried to go back to sleep. A fruitless effort. Sleep wasn't Matter's friend at the best of times, and this was certainly not that. Their stupid brain was far too awake for sleep anyway, since it was perfectly unaffected by the pain pressing against the rest of them. Except not completely unaffected, the negativity was…

Matter sighed, imagining what Brruuh would say if they admitted to feeling utterly useless whenever their symptoms flared. Would he be kind and patient, offer tools Matter had already tried and discarded? Or would he be frustrated, like that one cognitivist who couldn't seem to understand that the problem was that, when flared, Matter genuinely couldn't do anything including basic self-care tasks? No. Brruuh wasn't the type to show frustration to a patient, to someone asking for his help. He'd offer tools and when they didn't work, he'd go looking for new ones. He'd probably keep looking until he found something, even if it took forever.

Their fingers hovered over the communications tab on their wristband, almost ready to call him.

And when those offered tools didn't work, Brruuh would get that little scrunch on his nose. And then he'd suggest leaning on their community, their Ahthae for help. Ick!

They swiped to the entertainment centre of their wristband instead. They had a few vids downloaded and, with just a little wrangling, they could tap into the entire crew's downloaded libraries. Basti always had a few weird but easy to follow oldies. And some twentieth-through-twenty-third century sci-fi nonsense, looking back at their hope for the future was always a fun time. Flip phones, and badge-based communicators, and other once-futuristic tech. Plus the doctor from that trekking one was cute.

Matter had made their way through most of season one when their door opened. They expected Sauraxen—or maybe Basti since they were hijacking his vids—nobody else on the crew would enter without knocking. But the wash of another ouaeahhn swept over them, setting them immediately on edge. They clenched their mental shields tighter around themself, the added pressure twisting their joints into agony they hadn't known possible.

They paused the vid; a model of the ship still projected on their ceiling, and rested fingers against the personal shields tucked up against that wristband.

Still there, still functioning. Still blocking most of their thoughts and feelings from this stranger even if their internal shields failed.

Shield tech was complicated for ouaeahhn, especially since it was ouaeahhn tech. Official IPA documentation said shield tech like this was 89% effective. In reality, it varied for ouaeahhn-ouaeahhn communication and among Ahthae. But nobody talked about that because no ouaeahhn wanted to admit that they had fudged the numbers to the IPA. It was almost impossible to explain the disparity to null species, those with no tele-empathetic conversation ability. Like trying to explain sounds to a deaf species, or texture to a touchless one, or breathing both under and over water to a species who could only do one of those.

"Ymmattrahni," the stranger greeted. He twisted their name up into its most negative version. No feeling of home among the stars, not even the accusative nature Chamber had hurled it at them with—more forgivable, her last experience before going into stasis had been war with Ouaeahhn after all—but this ouaeahhn before them sneered it like it was the inevitable downfall of Matter's whole world. Their own doing, their own destruction wrought over the people they most cared for.

Matter said nothing. Waited. Wanting to shove up into the slightly less vulnerable position of sitting but knowing better than to display their pain like that.

They might have grown up on ouaeahhn, where vulnerability was negligible, but they were still half human. And this ouaeahhn was…

"Low contact?" he asked in Ouaeahhn.

Still Matter said nothing.

"Hnanttrouse." It came with a strong wave of emotion that left no questions as to the most accurate translation of that name, even in a language as emotionally malleable as ouaeahhn. People breaker and alone maker.

"Nei offence," Matter said finally, sticking to the safe distance of ECE. "But I'd really rather not do this now. This is a human run ship, closed doors mean privacy." That wasn't just a human system, it was IPA standard unless stated otherwise. And even then, most no-privacy crews didn't bother with the doors at all.

"Nei such thing as privacy on Ouaeahhn."

"We're not on Ouaeahhn."

"Nei such thing as privacy *for* ouaeahhn either."

Dimae

Dimae was most of the way through unpacking the medical supplies from the crate, grateful to be more focused this time than when he had been trying to catalogue and getting lost in a timeless void, when

Matter surged into medi-bay, slamming the door closed behind them. Such a different entrance to their normal reluctance that Dimae literally dropped what was in his hands, medicine spilling all over the floor, to focus every piece of attention onto Matter as they slid to the floor with a grimace twisting their face.

His ears twitched to pick up their rapid heartbeat, their huffing breaths. What was it that brought them here when they normally waited out pain that would show this visibly on their face? They couldn't be out of meds already, not unless this was an overdose and that typically looked different to this.

"I…" they trailed off, holding the space whale Brruuh had made in one tight fist at their side. Their customary jumpsuit was absent, replaced by a blanket held on it seemed by the collective willpower of Dimae and Matter.

"You?" Dimae prompted, crouching by them. He got no response. "Medical thing?"

"Nei. Ja. I don't know."

"May I help you onto the medi-bed?"

"Please."

He placed each touch with care, wrapping arms around Matter in an impertinent way to spread the pressure of lifting them onto the medical bed. Minimising the pain where he could.

"I am having a medical thing," Matter explained as they leaned back against the wall behind the bed, fingers turning soft against the woven whale. "But I'm here for something else."

Dimae waited for them to explain, automatically setting the medi-scanner running. Unsurprisingly it showed elevated levels of stress, muscle stiffness and weakness. It read like a human heart attack, but Matter was too ouaeahhn for that.

They tilted their head to rest on the wall too, exposing their throat to him. "Would you sit?"

Not the first time Matter had made the odd request, nor the first time Dimae had acquiesced. His first job was always his patients' health and comfort, even if it was weird.

"Basti invited a passenger aboard from the pit stop."

"My nose told me as much," Dimae agreed.

"He's ouaeahhn but he's... We call it Ma-se: a single traveller, but it's..." they huffed out a breath. "The feeling behind the title is, I guess disapproving is a good word. Ouaeahhn prioritises community above all. It doesn't matter who you find community with, as long as you have one. Hnanttrouse—the passenger, the Ma-se, is someone who chooses not to bond."

"You are uncomfortable with his presence here." But why come to Dimae about it? Because he was Basti's husband and ostensibly second in command? Trying to convince him to get Basti to drop off this passenger sooner rather than later?

"Ja, but that's not why I'm in medi-bay. Well, it is, but not the way I think you're thinking."

"What do you think I'm thinking?"

"That I'm being a prejudiced asshole."

A laugh burst out of Dimae.

"I try not to have a problem with Ma-se, I don't have any room to talk about shifting in and out of communities, about living alone and liking my privacy. I mean this one in particular is refusing to abide by standard IPA privacy boundaries, so I feel like I'm justified in my dislike here. But I'm not here in medi-bay because I don't like the guy. Well, I am but, I wanted to ask you a favour."

"Go ahead."

"Harrushetti aren't just tele-empathically null, you're tele-empathically shielded, hard to reach. Being around you makes every other tele-empathic connection just a little more difficult."

Like a signal shield, a radius that prevented tele-empathic readings.

"Just while Hnanttrouse is here, could I stick to you? Not literally, it's an—"

"Idiom, I know. Basti has used it before." He'd never considered being a safety net for anyone other than Basti. Even if it was only for a piece of his intrinsic nature that he had no control over. "You want me to be your personal protector?"

"My personal shield, yeah. Would that be completely unreasonable?"

"Why me? Why not Brruuh?"

"Brruuh is great too. But you're more resilient

against tele-empathy. And you have this lovely hidey-hole here with known, ouaeahhn-proof privacy rules."

Dimae's ears flicked but he kept his mouth shut. Privacy was important on Harrush, but that didn't mean it was so common elsewhere. Then again, if Matter was complaining about a lack of privacy, it must have held significance to them too. And obviously, it did not occur to the passenger.

"I can go and ask Brruuh if you're not comfy," Matter offered. "In a minute… or five."

"Don't worry about it. I can provide that medical care. If you rest for now."

Matter's smile was weak as Dimae moved back to continue unpacking. The next time he turned around, they were asleep on the medi-bed. He would need to have a conversation with his Bond Mate about passengers. This was a cargo ship for a start and, more importantly, this was the home of every member of the crew, inviting an unvetted stranger into that was neither fair nor reasonable.

Travel

Day 5

Brruuh

The presence of another ouaeahhn on the ship made the translucent sheen on Matter's skin shimmer a little brighter, like a puddle of oil beneath a ship's leaking engine. They sat at the table in the aufenthaltsraum, in their regular spot next to the head of the table, close enough to use the coffee machine without rising.

The other ouaeahhn sparkled in the artificial light, brighter and more reflective than Matter, with their human father, could ever be. He reflected the green, white, and pops of colour from the botany area in the back of the aufenthaltsraum, the shining silver of the kitchen appliances, and the odd mix of LeaYaPar golds and TeaYaBin greys that covered the sofas. He had taken up a spot opposite Matter, setting his back against the sofa-zone.

Brruuh squeezed past Dimae, in the chair next to Matter, whose ears were so flat you could have balanced a tray on top of them. Brruuh's eyes flicked between the two ouaeahhn in the room. Which one of them had upset Dimae that much?

Harrushetti and ouaeahhn notoriously didn't get along. Harrushetti planetary culture was closed, prudish, private. Their family units bonded tightly and often rejected outsiders, even potential Bond Mates, whether they were also harrushetti or not. Ouaeahhn, on the other hand, was built around the concept of connection, willing to welcome anyone with literally open arms. And that was the most basic aspect of the animosity between the two cultures. Each dealt with their negativity quietly for the most part, a subtle avoidance since IPA regulations didn't allow in-fighting.

Matter and Dimae often found themselves at odds with this culture clash at the base of it. But Matter wasn't the only ouaeahhn aboard now…

"I was worried," the new ouaeahhn said. "When your captain told me your full name but, as far as I see, it doesn't fit you. Ymmattrahni: destroyer of homes."

Brruuh's fingers spasmed around the plate he had grabbed, sending it crashing to the floor.

By the time he turned around, Matter's shoulders had pinched together with tension.

Dimae's ears perked toward the ouaeahhn. "Excuse me?"

"Ymmattrahni: danger, movement, and the feeling of home. How else would you translate that but homewrecker?"

Matter pushed to their feet, catching Brruuh with their arm and laying a soft apologetic hand briefly against the point of connection, as they squished around him toward the door of the aufenthaltsraum. He wanted to follow them, wanted to hear what else the other ouaeahhn had to say, and he wanted to be able to eat his food in peace. But he couldn't pick all three.

"Homewrecker?" Dimae asked.

Brruuh couldn't help the low growl that emanated from him. That wasn't a fair thing to call Matter. And it certainly wasn't right for Dimae to ask it like it made sense.

"That's my interpretation." The ouaeahhn turned his face toward Brruuh. "I'm Hnan, I don't think we've met."

"What does that translate to?" Brruuh demanded.

"Disconnected from my planet. I'm a traveller."

"You travel alone? That's rare for a ouaeahhn." How could one manage meaningful contact when travelling alone?

Hnan's lips pressed together. "Balancing my own ideas with someone else's… isn't my strongest skill."

Brruuh nodded slowly. He couldn't call himself surprised, what with the acrid scent of irritation that lingered where Matter had walked. Deciding to raise a cruel translation of someone's name after one of their Ahthae—their crew and found family entered the room—didn't paint a picture of politeness or community spirit.

Eating in his office went against Brruuh's stern work-life boundaries, the same boundaries that pressed against him in the aufenthaltsraum when it was used for something other than aufenthalts, but Brruuh grabbed snack foods from the cupboard instead of cooking and retreated to his private space anyway.

He found himself hiding in his office until the shifting of the lights signalled the night cycle starting on the ship. And then he found himself outside Sauraxen's door, hand already raised to knock when she emerged from the gravity well. Her head tilted backward in a wrexi smile when she noticed him.

"You're here early," she greeted.

"Rough day," Brruuh admitted. He had been trying to go through his notes and build an arsenal of evidence for being able to travel immediately without waiting for official permission. Instead, he'd ended up digging through ouaeahhn language again, getting frustrated when he couldn't grasp the core elements of the linguistic base—tele-empathetic languages were always going to be impossible to him but at least he could try for something better than he currently had.

He had at least been able to find a detailed description of the probable meaning behind eaahla: a term most commonly used for the thing that drew ouaeahhn attention. The thing around which the planet or person begins to orbit. That which shines brighter than all others. To Brruuh, that sounded like love, but all his research taught him love could come in many forms. And Matter had chosen to translate it as 'best friend' so that was that. A friend who drew their attention above others. Even if the worried, isolated part of him prickled at the possibility of other interpretations.

Sauraxen let him into her room, herding him into the bed and settling the curtains around them. Their own little world, with every noise from the ship beyond muted by fabric. There was something so wonderful about that falsified safety. About only him and Sauraxen being allowed within.

"Do you want to talk about it?" Sauraxen asked.

Brruuh shook his head, pressing his nose against Sauraxen's scales and inhaling deeply. Her scent hadn't changed with their passenger.

Underneath him, she giggled, squirrelling her hands under his jumper to stroke fingers over his skin.

Brruuh trailed his own hands over her shoulders, sliding the straps of her playsuit off her shoulders to allow her to wriggle out of it. He followed the fabric's movements, revelling in the warm softness of her scales. Chasing both with his nose and mouth, offering kisses to her skin.

Sauraxen tipped onto her back, letting out a little whine of pleasure that sent a thrill through Brruuh. A thrill he wanted to braid and weave into itself and into more.

Matter

Sleep had never exactly been Matter's best friend, but the tension suffusing the ship prickled against their nerves like an itchy blanket, forcing them to shift and shuffle in a desperate attempt to lessen that endless irritating sensation. It wasn't like they hadn't tried to sleep, their body crying out for rest, for an attempt to ease their pain. But every time they closed their eyes, their heart began thundering in their chest, rampaging around like a bee in a bottle. So they pushed out of bed, almost tossing a blanket over their shoulder in a traditionally ouaeahhn way, but swapping for a jumpsuit when they remembered Hnan was still aboard. At least he was in his own room for now.

Dipping into the corridor, the lights low on their night cycle rotation, Matter hesitated at the trilling sort of peep. Easy enough to shrug off as a Sauraxen noise—wrexi did peep—but Matter knew Sauraxen's peep: her shuffling sleep noise, her trying to be quiet noise, her frustrated one, the ones she made to encourage more of exactly that, and a thousand or more others learnt over a lifetime of friendship. They'd even started learning the language. And this peep wasn't right. It wasn't one of hers. So Matter scanned the corridor, searching out the source.

Too high pitched for a harrushetti, and Sebastian would never be able to close his throat tightly enough to create that kind of noise with his wide EC.623 accent. Even Hnan was an unlikely source, with ouaeahhn language as melodic as it was.

But it was definitely organic. Definitely something Matter had heard before. Something about it tickled like home, but when home was a threat rather than a promise.

Niahym.

Something brushed against their bare foot on the metal floor. Warm where the rest of them was cold. Soft where the metal was hard.

Letting out an unhinged shriek, Matter's foot retracted fast and hard enough to land a solid kick to their standing knee. They crashed into the nearest quarter's door. Sauraxen's.

On another ship that door might have crashed open, as it was it just made an unhealthy amount of noise. And pain. Oh, stars, that door was hard against Matter's already battered body. Had their shoulder capsized or was that only sensation?

When they could see past the pain again, they examined the thing where their feet had so recently been. A fluffy ball of a thing in sparking red-purple. "Ymnya," Matter breathed.

The door beneath their shoulder gave way, sending them crashing into something else solid. The fluff beneath that solid jerked Matter upright, except their legs still weren't ready to hold them. Strong hands gripped their shoulders, preventing them from falling and forcing a hissed breath out between their teeth. Brruuh's grip jerked but he didn't let go until Matter was steady on their feet again.

"What's wrong?" Sauraxen asked from behind him.

"Is that a nooknook?" Matter squeaked, eyes glued to the fluffy thing in the hallway.

"A what?"

"Ymnya! A nooknook!" the repetition came out more panicked.

Brruuh approached the fluffy thing slowly.

"Careful," Matter hissed. "It's Ymnya in

ouaeahhn—dangerous and fluffy. Nooknook in IPA standard." They were notoriously dangerous, a species that had invaded Ouaeahhn and become one of their only predators. They drew you in with cute noises and fluffiness, then latched on with the surprising teeth kept hidden beneath.

"It's a fluff pet," Hnan snarled, yanking his own door open. He grabbed the fluffy thing. "They're harmless. I'm nei idiot, I wouldn't transport nooknooks across the galaxy."

"You think you can lie to me?" Matter spat back. "I can tell, it seeps out of you like anla." A miasma, like water evaporating off a warm body in the early morning on EC.623—a visible mist with twirling lines.

Hnan rolled his eyes. "Sometimes nooknooks get caught up with them, but it's not like there's anything I could do to prevent that. Most people have never even heard of a nooknook."

"So they don't know to be careful. That's your defence?"

"You told us you were just travelling." Brruuh's voice was calm but firm. Matter hadn't heard that voice since their first meeting when they had teased him a little too far. "Are you telling us you are trading these creatures?"

"It's legal."

"With a license, perhaps."

"I don't need a license to trade within IPA space,

I'm an IPA citizen."

"You need a license if the thing you're trading is alive," Sauraxen argued. "Otherwise it's trafficking. You need proof that those creatures you're trading aren't actually people."

Hnan folded his arms. "That's ridiculous. If they were people they would have protested by now."

"You know their language, then?" Brruuh asked.

"What are you going to do about any of this?" Hnan snapped instead of answering.

"We could report you," Brruuh said, but there was a hesitancy there. They couldn't. They would get stuck in more IPA wait-stations as they dealt with not only Hnan, but the fact that Galactic Whale had left Station Gnarresh-Fle without official permission. And, on top of that, the fact that they had picked up a passenger while travelling semi-illegally. A passenger who was, apparently, trafficking not-nooknooks.

"It's Basti's decision," Matter said.

"I'm pretty sure he's going to let it go," Hnan said, snide confidence pouring off him and wending its way past all of Matter's shields. "Since I fixed your little problem."

"Excuse me?"

"The magic of contact with another ouaeahhn."

A soft growl emanated from Brruuh.

"It doesn't work like that," Matter said, voice flat. "I have to give a shit about the people I'm in contact with. They have to make me feel good."

"That's not normal, you know that, right?"

Matter's hands fisted at their sides. The urge to hit something bubbling through them. No, not something, Hnan.

It was the human in them. The nature of a species designed to survive anything through a combination of collaboration and conflict. The rage and violence not something Matter had felt from any other ouaeahhn. It served well more often than not, offered a weight behind their sense of justice, their more protective instincts. But every coin had two sides.

"I think it's best if we all just go back to bed for now," Brruuh suggested, despite the growl still carrying under his words. He stepped between Matter and Hnan, placing himself directly in the line of all Matter's rage. "We can deal with this in the day-cycle."

Hnan retreated to his bedroom, sliding the door closed behind him. So much for no such thing as privacy for ouaeahhn.

"Come on," Sauraxen invited, tugging Matter by the waist. She led them into her room, unzipping their jumpsuit with the ease borne of practise and snuggling them into her bed without fuss.

Brruuh lingered in the doorway, let out a small huff, and turned to leave.

Travel
Day 6

Brruuh

Brruuh had taken up a place on the catwalk stairs over the cargo bay. With much deliberation, he had picked the stairs closest to engineering rather than the ones directly outside the captain's quarters. He wasn't trying to cause trouble, didn't want to make anyone feel ambushed, just wasn't willing to wait to happen to run into the captain. Brruuh had been willing to put up with the tension, had been willing to get to work to help the crew through it as their resident cognitivist. He had done research, started making his office inviting for Matter if they needed to talk through and settle things. He'd even retreated to his own room to leave Sauraxen and Matter alone in her bed—a bed he was quickly coming to claim as one of his—despite the way it made jealousy twist inside him to be ousted like that. But after last night, after the discovery of the mysterious creatures living aboard the ship, the risk Hnan created outweighed Brruuh's ability to solve interpersonal relationship issues.

Sebastian emerged from his quarters, halfway to pulling his cloud of coily hair into its usual pineapple atop his head. "Brruuh?" he asked.

"Captain," Brruuh greeted.

"Is this a pre-coffee conversation?"

Brruuh held out an insulated flask of coffee.

"Alright, where shall we meet?"

"There's my office," Brruuh offered. If they were willing to walk through the living floor of the ship. Which Brruuh was somewhat reluctant to allow. Too high risk of running into another member of the crew or Hnan. Too high risk of being delayed, or being asked what they were doing.

"Or medi-bay," Basti suggested. "Dimae won't be up for a while."

Brruuh's eyes flicked over Basti's head to the door behind him. Harrushetti rested in bursts totalling about six hours spread throughout a day, very different from the human inclination to sleep for a solid seven to ten hours. Dimae shouldn't need more sleep than his human husband. Was Dimae's recovery going that slowly? Brruuh barely had any lingering physical problems, his fur would take a little while to settle back to what it had been before, and emotionally he was... working on emotionally recovering.

Saying nothing about it for now, Brruuh started down the catwalk stairs.

"Okay," Basti said, hopping onto the medi-bed and sipping at the coffee Brruuh had brought him. "What's up?"

"Hnan."

Basti grimaced.

"He's illegally transporting goods."

"Goods like…?"

"Living creatures intended to be pets."

Basti closed his eyes and took a breath, then set the coffee on the bed next to him and dropped his head into his hands, loosing a groan.

"We have options," Brruuh said when the noise ceased.

"We'll drop him off early," Basti said.

Brruuh nodded. "I think Matter is already picking out planets to dispose of him on."

Sebastian laughed ruefully. "Habitable ones?"

Brruuh's ears flicked with amusement. "Presumably. They're struggling a lot with your decision regarding Hnan."

"What do you mean?"

"He's mentioned—repeatedly mentioned—that you brought another ouaeahhn aboard to 'fix their problem'. And he is… quite rude."

"Ja, the only other ouaeahhn I'd met properly before was Matter, I thought they would all be like them."

"That's very—"

"I know it's bad!" Basti interrupted. "Nobody can be the epitome of their people like that and even if they could there's always exceptions." He sighed. "I thought he needed help."

"That's admirable. But as captain you have to be more aware of what these kinds of decisions will do to your crew. Bringing aboard a ouaeahhn without asking your ouaeahhn crew is… generally a poor choice." Especially on a ship not designed for passengers, but Brruuh didn't want to start piling on problems when Basti already stank of guilt. "You are a good captain, Basti, I've observed enough bad ones to know. Your—what's the human phrase?—heart is in the middle?"

"Heart is in the right place," Basti suggested.

Brruuh held in his scoff at the idiom, hearts were usually in the right place, weren't they? And the right place for a human heart was in the middle, if the way they kept putting their hands over it when they had big emotions was anything to go by. "That. You care for your crew, you balance your ship needs. This is one mistake to learn from."

"You're right. I'll go talk to Matter." He slid to his feet, grabbing the coffee again.

"Before you do."

Basti stopped.

"You know I am here for your emotional wellbeing."

"I know."

Brruuh gave him a significant look.

Basti ducked his head. "I'll try to be better at asking for it."

Brruuh found himself huffing again. If any crew needed a cognitivist available full time it was this one.

Sauraxen

Sauraxen woke with Matter's distinctive scent and presence wrapped around her like a blanket. She stretched and snuggled into them. "I've missed this," she murmured.

"Me too." There was a hesitation to the statement. A hesitation that turned into, "It's not going to cause tension with Brruuh, is it?"

Sauraxen shrugged. "If it does we'll deal with it." Her closeness with Matter had been an issue for previous partners but, despite harrushetti hyper-monogamy, Brruuh didn't seem to have much of an issue so far.

Matter flopped onto their back, staring up at the ceiling of Sauraxen's quarters. "Can I stay here for a bit?"

"Worried about running into Hnan?"

"For sure."

Something about it made Sauraxen think there might be more than just that, but when she left room for Matter to say more, they didn't. "I'll bring you some food," she offered, scuttling out of the bed.

"You're the best."

The aufenthaltsraum, already bright and scented with the bitter delicious tang of coffee, was empty when Sauraxen entered. She flipped the lights to her preferred level and made her way over to the designated kitchen area.

Cooking for Matter was often a weird experience. They had some foods in common: pizza pockets, biscuits, rice with toppings, and other similar human-origin food. But it was still strange to cook for them. Sauraxen had never been set to cooking duty amongst the wrexi, too busy focusing on various engineering projects to be pulled away like that. Everybody knew she had plans to study on an IPA station and find a life amongst the stars, teaching her Pitzk-focused duties seemed pointless in the face of that. Still, cooking for Matter evoked some of that feeling, that community memory she had barely started to build before she left.

The soft undercurrent thread of a conversation Sauraxen couldn't hear illuminated the open areas of the ship even as Sauraxen clattered too loudly in the kitchen for the words to be clear. Someone was talking in the cargo bay. The pilot's console door was closed—a rarity, but with Hnan being so abrasive it made sense that Matter might choose to keep their domain private. The engines ticked away quietly below Sauraxen, moving the way they should. Taking them home to Pitzk. To her vava.

Sauraxen pulled her hair tighter around her again, seeking comfort that probably wasn't coming. She wanted to send another message, wanted more information than vava had given. Wanted to know she wasn't already too late. But the message would get there and sit in that fucking communications tower until someone went to get it, and she would have to wait for them to return to send out a reply, which meant there was absolutely no point sending anything at all.

The clatter of the catwalk, the hum of the gravity well, and Brruuh stepped into the aufenthaltsraum the same silent way he moved everywhere. He chirped a greeting, sliding arms around Sauraxen's waist. She leaned her head back against him, hair snaking over his arms thoughtlessly.

He rubbed his chin against the top of her head. "You okay after last night?" he asked.

"Well enough."

"Matter?"

"Still in my room. We might hang out today."

"Alone?"

"Depends on whether you want to sit through old human vids about space travel."

"Like history?"

"Like fiction from before they'd mastered intergalactic travel."

"Hope punk?"

"More or less. It's what was shared out of their wristband." The vid had been paused at some point and Matter hadn't yet thought to return to it to either close it or keep playing. On rough days like this, vids were a lifeline.

"I liked the last human vid I watched with them," Brruuh said. That had been in their original assessment, well before Brruuh had told Sauraxen about any feelings, possibly before he realised he had any. Matter had felt rough, so they'd lounged on the sofas in the aufenthaltsraum, projecting an old vid onto the plain wall, a rom-com about a young woman exceeding the expectations placed upon her. Not hugely similar to the then-futuristic space vids. But not completely incomparable either.

"Great." Sauraxen tilted her chin up at him. "Help me put this in a bowl?" She could see it, but it was far easier for a visual creature to manage the transfer of the intricacies of pouring food from one container to another. Wrexi used large spoons on Pitzk—maybe she should get a ladle.

Retreating to her room with two coffees, a full packet of biscuits, and a bowl of what Basti would term 'real food'—as if that was a legitimate designation—and Brruuh hot on her heels, Sauraxen peeped before she opened the door.

"Nei clothes," Brruuh murmured.

"My room," Sauraxen huffed back, slithering out of her own t-shirt so oversized it fell to her knees and barely stayed on her shoulders. She'd only put it on to go into the aufenthaltsraum. She offered a Wrexi question to Matter, asking if it was okay to let Brruuh through the doorway.

Matter chirruped back in poorly pronounced Wrexi, an affirmative but a dubious one.

"Am I allowed to keep mine on?" Brruuh asked, oblivious to their private conversation.

On the bed, Matter burst into laughter, tension melting away with it even as they tugged a blanket over their midsection. "Room owner's choice."

Sauraxen hummed as if deep in thought, climbing onto the bed, waiting until Brruuh's ears twitched. "For now."

Brruuh scrunched his nose, huffing a short breath out of it either for emphasis or to make it clear to Sauraxen that an expression was happening. But he climbed onto the bed with the pair of them, settling half against the wall. "What are we watching?"

"One of Basti's vids," Matter said. "A series."

"You can catch me up?"

Matter let the vid play on the curtains surrounding Sauraxen's bed, pausing at various moments to point out characters and explain who they were and how they had come to be at this point in the story. Brruuh hummed attentively at each one, regardless of the disruption to the viewing, or the fact that Matter had explained one particular character three times already.

Travel
Day 7

Sauraxen

Standing in the shadows of engineering, the rattle of the boarding plank washed over Sauraxen, illuminating the surrounding area. Waking up with Matter two mornings in a row had been a surprise, something she hadn't expected to feel again after starting her relationship with Brruuh, who had let himself out at some point, though Sauraxen couldn't have said when. She and Matter had spent a luxurious amount of time snuggling together, Matter's warm scent comforting as always.

Still, both of them had been wrangling their thoughts about Hnan, about his actions and attitude. Sauraxen hadn't spent much time with him, but as a member of a species often taken to be a pet, she had little patience for creature-traders. Matter had gone to take them into land somewhere to drop him off, walking stiffly but with even steps out of Sauraxen's room in one of the intricately woven jumpers she'd thiefed from Brruuh. Wriggling into a jumpsuit was probably too painful an experience after bashing their shoulder against the door the way they had the night with the nooknook or whatever it was. And, left alone, Sauraxen had decided to seclude herself in the darkness of engineering, ready to observe Hnan leaving.

Each step Hnan took off the ship was like a weight lifting from her shoulders. She would always have been uncomfortable having a stranger on the ship, really. Prey species. But the way Hnan had behaved put everyone ill-at-ease.

Basti, the only person who had officially come to see Hnan off the ship, clicked the button to close the boarding plank and the soft hum of it retreating filled the space. When the ship was closed and Basti had sent the message to Matter that they could set off again, Sauraxen slipped out of the shadows with a soft peep.

Basti sighed. "I really thought…"

"Thought what?"

"I thought it was a good idea. Like he would have helped."

"Helped with?"

"Money. Matter."

"What's wrong with Matter?"

Basti let out a little snort. He didn't believe Sauraxen couldn't figure that out for herself. He wasn't exactly wrong. Sauraxen knew Matter well enough to recognise that they had been having more pain days. But apparently Basti wasn't so content to wait and see if they improved on their own. The same patience he was apparently offering to Brruuh and Dimae. Why was Matter different? Because they had a chronic illness with no cure? Because they had already been struggling before the events of Clickclick? That wasn't exactly fair, Matter managed themself perfectly fine. Sure, they needed accommodations, but accommodations were part and parcel of IPA expectations, why would that be different just because it was illness-based rather than species or planet based?

"If Matter wanted to meet with another ouaeahhn, they would raise that themself," Brruuh's voice called from the top of the catwalk.

Sauraxen let out a little trill at his surprise presence. He offered a soft hum of apology.

"You don't get it!" Basti argued.

"What is there to get?" Brruuh closed the hatch

between the cargo bay and the living floor. Enclosing this conversation in the cavernous space, an attempt to prevent the words from echoing up to Matter's ears.

"Matter is sick," Sebastian huffed.

"We all know they have a chronic condition."

"It's getting worse."

Sauraxen swiped a hand over her eyes, once again wishing the people around her better understood wrexi non-verbal communication. She'd noticed. She'd have to be exceedingly self-involved not to.

"You have to trust them to come to you if they need help," Brruuh said.

"You didn't see them there, you didn't have to go to—" Basti cut himself off.

Sauraxen reached out to touch a hand to his arm. She could imagine it.

Processing dynamic, sarcastic, and passionate Brruuh lying in that hospital bed had been horrible. It was wrong to see someone clinging so fragilely to life. Especially someone usually so bright. Basti had been through the same thing with Dimae. And before that, back however many years ago he had also been the one to go and pick up Matter when they had been rescued from the trafficking ring.

"It's just weighing on me," Basti admitted. "All of it."

Sauraxen's hand retracted. Death hung over this whole journey, from their start to their end. And she hadn't considered how difficult it might be for the rest of the crew to partake in this journey with her. How much it might bring up the troubles they had faced in their own lives.

Brruuh losing his whole family and community. Matter's experience with trafficking. Basti's experience of always being the one to bounce back and take care of everyone.

"Nei," Brruuh interrupted before anyone could say anything more. "If you have questions about Matter's wellbeing, ask them. Don't whisper about it behind their back. There is nothing worse than knowing everybody in your community is talking about the horrible thing that happened to you. I am happy to help you work through your own emotions about it. But if you're worried about Matter, you need to ask them, or trust them."

Travel Day 8

Sebastian

"Hey papa," Basti greeted into the wristband, not waiting for the holo-pixels to form into the shape of his father's face. He'd shut the door to his quarters and taken a seat on the huge bed, soft blankets surrounding him. He trailed fingers through one of them, picking out the places where different weaves meshed together.

Dimae had put together their bed—what he

called their nest. Layers of cushions and blankets piled atop each other and the mattress large enough to easily fit five Basti-sized people on it. It was important to have a 'scent soaked' place to return to, somewhere that smelled like the both of them. The struggle of managing human cleaning needs and harrushetti scent needs was still a work in progress at times. They'd spent enough years separated by entire galaxies that they'd only needed to start finding a permanent solution after deciding to go all in on Galactic Whale. But Basti couldn't imagine sleeping on a traditional, one-to-two layer bed anymore. Couldn't imagine sleeping without Dimae by his side.

"Hey kiddo," Jonesy greeted. "What do you need?"

"What do you mean by that?"

Jonesy laughed, his smile so much like Basti's own. The older he got the more he looked like his father. Smile and frown lines developing in the same places. Hair turning greyer the same way Jonesy's had. "You only ever call if you need something."

Basti grimaced. "Oops?"

"How's the ship? How's Dimae? And… Everyone else?"

"We're fixing up pretty okay. Dimae is… He says he's fine."

"Like you said you were fine when you fell out of that tree and we had to rebreak your leg?"

"Ja, like that." Basti sighed. "Sauraxen's vava—her primary parent—is sick, so we got medical dispensation to travel to Pitzk." It was only a little lie.

"Oh, kiddo, that sucks. Share whatever is the wrexi-appropriate consolations from me, okay?"

"Will do," Basti promised. They lapsed into silence. This had been a bad idea. Why did he think calling papa was wise?

"I'm okay," Jonesy reassured.

"Huh?"

"I'm okay. I'm healthy and well. So is your sister, I talked to her last week—she actually calls on a regular basis."

Basti rolled his eyes performatively.

"We're all fine, the farm is good. I've got a new farmhand, can you believe it, an alien moved here! Name of Kibash, has eight limbs like a spider and can use up to six of them as hands or feet at any given time. Freaks the other hands out sometimes, but she's so efficient that I don't care."

Basti laughed.

"I'd take seven Kibash's over getting you back on the farm."

"Are you trying to say I wasn't an efficient member of the team?"

"Ja, that's exactly what I'm saying. You spent so much time thinking about history or exploring the stars. And then when Matter turned up you were gone."

"I didn't leave for another two years."

Jonesy shook his head. "You had an in for the IPA,

the type your mama could never provide. And, more importantly, you had another person who also couldn't think of another path but the stars."

"Speaking of Matter, you talk to them lately?"

"They're on your ship."

Not an answer, but Basti didn't say that. He didn't say anything.

"Come on, Sebastian, don't give me a hard time about this."

"I'm not. I just think they might benefit from your stories about Kibash."

Jonesy looked away from Basti. He wouldn't be able to see the rest of the captains' quarters no matter how much it seemed like he was looking at the folding chair set up in front of the desk built into the wall. He must be looking at something in his own environment. Was he in the house? Sat in his favourite chair and avoiding Basti's gaze by looking out over the farmland? Or was he outside and surrounded by crops? "They've stopped answering my calls. The only way I know they're still alive is you'd tell me if they weren't."

"How do you cope with that?"

Jonesy shrugged. "Ajo y agua. I know I had my part in it." He looked at Basti again. "Whether I can change or not doesn't matter if they're not willing to reach back, you know?"

Basti nodded slowly. Ajo y agua, skase kai kolumpa, no matter how you got there, it was the situation you were in, your fault and your responsibility to get out of. Maybe he *should* book a cognitivism session with Brruuh. "I don't think I know how to swim out of this," Basti admitted.

"You're in trouble?"

"Kinda."

"You've got me, your mama, and an entire crew at your back. You can figure your way out of this too."

"You don't even know what trouble I'm in."

"I don't need to. I know you, Sebastian. You're creative and caring and you're always trying your best to do the right thing. What did I always say?"

"Don't be like me, be yourself, it's better?"

"You're a little shit."

Basti laughed. "Whether you can change or not, apologise. If you can reasonably change, try to. And you're always allowed to explain your thought process."

"There you go then."

"T'aime, papa."

"T'aime, kiddo."

With the call ended, Jonesy's holographic face disappeared from view, Basti made his way to the pilot's console. He lingered in the doorway, watching as Matter expertly shifted the ship through the void. Stars passed at dizzying speeds outside the dome, a wash of colour and light that always left Basti reeling.

"I don't smell coffee," Matter called over their shoulder, not looking away from their trajectory.

"I have something else."

They glanced back, eyes still glittering with the galaxy beyond. "What?"

"An apology."

"Ew, I don't want that."

Basti laughed. "Can I give it to you anyway?"

Matter turned back to the dome with a smile. "I only accept apologies in the form of coffee, cake, or chilli."

"Not cuddles?"

"Hmm, I suppose I could be convinced. But probably not while I'm working."

"Any chance autopilot could handle it for a bit? This is serious."

"Like I told Brruuh, I don't take things seriously."

Basti laughed again. "You're not making this easy."

"All the best things are difficult."

"I'm sorry!" Basti joke shouted.

Matter laughed, shifting in their chair to turn their whole body toward him.

"I was an idiot and a real Jonesy about it."

"Think you know best?"

"I am my father's son."

"What did you know best about this time?"

"Everything, I think. But especially you."

"That is a real Jonesy move."

"I should have asked you, and I am asking you now."

Matter tensed, reflections fading as they braced

themself to close off. Stars, how had he never noticed that before?

"Do you need anything?"

"Like what?"

"A hover chair? A cuddle? Coffee?"

"I hate that you did that without me."

"What?"

"The hover chair. If I wanted one, if I needed one, I could request one from the IPA, I could get my own one that's exactly what I want it to be. I could even choose to spend my own money on it. You might not pay me well but other people have and I'm not extravagant." They sighed. "You pushed me into having one and now it's hard to decide if I need it without getting mixed up with the frustration."

"I'll try to be better about that."

"But you're still Basti, still my captain and my Ahthae and my family. You're never going to be able to stop being overprotective, even if you are a little brother."

"Hey! It's different for us." Because, despite Matter existing in the universe longer, ouaeahhn matured at a slower rate, lived far longer than humans, and Basti had lapped them in equivalent ages.

"My point is that it's in your nature to try to fix problems before they start. It makes you a good captain but it makes you a shitty friend sometimes."

"That's fair. Do you want me to get rid of the hover chair?"

"Give it to Dimae as a medical thing. Who knows what shenanigans we're going to get ourselves into over the years. It's not a bad idea to have something like that in the ship's storage. Just don't make it mine." They turned back to the dome, fingers settling over the controls again. "And bring me coffee."

Travel
Day 10

Getting to the edge of Pitzk after depositing Hnan at another fuel stop proved surprisingly quick. Although Dimae couldn't have said how much of that was Matter getting back into the pilot's console rather than hiding in their room or hovering near him to use his tele-empathic shielding.

He had grown accustomed to the regular bleep-bleep of their wristband reminding them to take more meds. He pulled medicine down from the cupboards, pieces he'd put together a thousand times, if not in this specific order. "I find myself frustrated," he said to Brruuh in harrushetti. He'd invited the cognitivist down to medi-bay as the swirl of Pitzk's galaxy appeared on his wristband's radar.

"At what?" Brruuh asked.

"Perhaps something illogical."

"Are you a Chluian now?"

Dimae laughed. He had visited a Chluian retreat as part of his medical education on Harrush. A group of harrushetti with a specific focus on becoming enlightened and most logical through meditation and emotional maintenance. The primary location of such people was the Chluian moon, which had lent the practise its name. Some of Dimae's fellow students had travelled to the moon for further study, choosing to incorporate teachings of logic into their medical practice like foundational lines in a weave. Dimae found the atmosphere of it, even the welcoming retreat, too restrictive, but Dimae had also ended up falling desperately in love with a human so he supposed that made sense. Humans and logic didn't tend to mix well.

"What are you frustrated with?" Brruuh prompted the whole phrase only a single chirrup in harrushetti.

"I am still struggling with recovery and I shouldn't be."

"Shouldn't?"

Cognitivists! "It doesn't make sense to be struggling with this. I am physically improved." Except for excess of sleep and some fuzziness to his fur. "Why do I still feel such bad emotions?"

"You nearly died. It's normal to feel strong feelings of some sort after the fact."

"And what are your strong feelings?" he spat the words like an accusation.

"Some people," Brruuh countered, "feel an excessive joy for life, seeking only positive experiences. Some people get stuck in melancholy. Ironically Chluian practices could help."

"Do not."

"Or, find something soothing to do. Let your brain process those feelings without needing to actively do the processing."

"What do you do?"

"Wool work. But that won't function for you, it would likely be a source of further frustration to try and learn right now. What do you always find yourself going back to?"

Dimae's ears twitched in thought. What did he find himself going back to? Medicine, but he doubted that would be an appropriate response considering it was his job. It sounded like it needed to be repetitive, something he could do with and without needing to focus.

"You don't have to tell me. You don't have to know now. But whatever it ends up being, *that* is the thing to lean on now."

The sting of sulphur invaded the conversation, the interruption enough to send it crashing to its end. They hadn't even landed yet and the atmospheric pressure let the substance seep through cracks that shouldn't exist in a ship that was space worthy.

Trying to shake off the sensation, Dimae double checked the assorted tools and medicines laid out in surgical precision on his rolling trolley before gesturing Brruuh into the cargo bay and dragging the trolley with him.

With all the crew lined up outside medi-bay, the cargo bay expansive around them, he could almost see himself as the military commander his ancestral line said he should have been. His grandparents had been so disappointed by his interest in healing rather than hurting. Grandmother, his riarch, had complained at every stage of Dimae's application to study and further study medicine. Sometimes he wondered if the semi-rejection of Basti was intrinsically tied into that disappointment. If Dimae hadn't studied medicine, he wouldn't have met this human with whom he had ultimately fallen in love.

Not that a harrushetti commander would likely have such a wildly assorted crew. A human with smooth brown skin and explosive hair, a tiny lizardoid with pearlescent scales, a YaBin harrushetti with kittenish mannerisms, and, worst of all, the glittering purple of an ouaeahhn.

"The atmosphere of Pitzk is inhospitable to most lifeforms," he explained. "I have meds that will prevent it from immediately killing you while we descend into the tunnels." He picked up a syringe from the trolley. "Which humanoid first?"

Basti backed away, whining, "In a shot? Nei. Whyyyyy?"

Matter rolled their eyes and slipped the shoulder of their jumpsuit off, revealing patterned skin beneath. Not like his own or Brruuh's fur based pattern, no, this was like scarring but in patterns. He shook off the interest, no need to sneeze in the face of a sleeping mrant with Matter's usual medical intervention resistance absent. He delivered the shot, a little of Matter's iridescent blood welling to the surface. Dimae wiped it away with a pre-prepared wipe.

"What's the plan for us?" Brruuh asked.

Dimae flicked his ears.

Brruuh let out a chirrup of apology.

"That's annoushaaah," Matter said to the other harrushetti.

Brruuh stuck his tongue out at them, a decidedly human and somehow kittenish gesture.

Dimae elected to ignore the confusing interaction and asked Matter, "You okay?"

Matter offered a very wide, very human smile that quickly turned to a grimace. "Oh, ew, why can I taste it? That's weird."

Dimae huffed a laugh and returned to the trolley to offer Brruuh a tablet. "As they say in ECE, cup bottoms up."

"Isn't it just 'bottoms up'?" Sauraxen asked.

"That would be inappropriate from one harrushetti to another, because a bottom can also be a body part," Brruuh clarified.

"That's the whole point of that saying," Matter interjected, levering themself to sit on the catwalk steps with a soft exhale that might as well have been a scream of pain.

Brruuh tipped the tablet into his mouth, letting out little 'ecks' when it didn't go down easily.

"Why do you two get tablets!?" Basti cried, hiding behind the handrail next to Matter.

"Because breaking a harrushetti's skin is dangerous."

"Dangerous how?" Sauraxen asked.

"Risk of shock. We're hard to hurt, but when hurt happens…" Dimae trailed off, brushing hands over his fur. Still frizzier than he was used to, leaving him looking more like his awkward teenage pictures than his usual sleek adult coat. He turned back to the trolley, busying himself with work instead of thinking about the cause of his tuftier fur.

His eyes flitted back over to Matter who had started an animated conversation with Brruuh about different kinds of apologies. They had managed to get used to a new normal more than once already. True, they were from two particularly adaptable species and Dimae was not, but he could change. He popped his own tablet into his mouth, swallowing with less fuss than Brruuh.

He grabbed the atomiser and turned to Sauraxen. She lifted her sensory hair to better absorb the twin sprays Dimae pressed over her.

"Why does Sauraxen get the spray version?" Basti whined. "Don't you love me?"

Matter snorted. "You big baby."

"It's a legitimate fear!" Basti protested.

"Annoushaaah. But—"

"I don't think you're meant to 'but' an annoushaaah," Brruuh complained.

"It's not your language, anea."

Brruuh gasped. "My ouaeahhn translator says you just called me a fun-breaker!"

Beside him, Sauraxen burst into a series of peeping laughs.

Matter turned back to Basti, "If a doctor as qualified as Dimae, who loves you as much as Dimae couldn't find another option for you, I doubt there is one."

"I did try," Dimae confirmed.

"Can't I just wear a space suit?" Basti asked.

"Sadly no," Sauraxen said, getting herself back under control. "The atmosphere on Pitzk is known to degrade the filters on space suits too quickly to get people deep enough into the tunnels. Even if you could manage, you, as a human, would still be too sensitive to the sulphur that does make it down there. Plus a suit wouldn't fit in the tunnels."

"How about this," Matter suggested. "Those two will go into engineering and get distracted." They waggled their eyebrows. "And you can bury your face in my neck while your extremely qualified husband handles the situation. You don't have to know anything about it."

Basti flung himself into Matter's arms, tucking his face tight against their neck.

Dimae pressed down on the swirl of jealousy that wanted to rear its head at the visible closeness of the pair and grabbed the syringe as Brruuh and Sauraxen disappeared through the door to engineering.

Sauraxen

The light from the nearby star stabbed at Sauraxen's eyes, burning what years of evolutions had designed to function best in dim tunnels. The presence of sulphur, yellow enough for even Sauraxen to see, pressed against her skin, further hampering her perception. The smell filled her lungs in that way that took days to soften and dissipate. Would they even be in the tunnels long enough for it to dissipate before returning to the ship?

Sauraxen scampered over to the nearest soothing seeming area, a cave entrance. Nobody lingered to greet them. Since Sauraxen was in the landing party, she was in charge of getting the crew into the tunnels to meet a welcoming party deep enough that they wouldn't suffer any adverse effects of the surface.

She just had to hope the others could follow without getting lost in the yellow clouds of the surface.

Inside the tunnels, Sauraxen shook off what she could of the yellow dust, letting it ploof into a little cloud around her. Basti let out a little cough and the two harrushetti copied her shake.

"All here?"

"One, two, three, four, five," Basti counted. "All here."

Sauraxen tilted her head back in a smile. That captaincy training rarely showed itself in traditional manner, but sometimes Basti came out with things straight out of the textbook.

Sauraxen turned to lead the way down the tunnels, sinking into the soothing cool darkness of her home. The sense of a small bundle of wrexi called her forward to find their greeting party. "Hello starbound one," the lead greeted in wrexi.

"Hello, home-keeping one," she replied.

"Should I have brought a translator?" Basti asked in a whisper.

"Nei," Sauraxen replied, swapping back to the language she spoke most often. "Most of us speak ECE, it's just a welcoming thing."

"Why do they know Earth Common Eurean, of all languages?" Brruuh asked, rumbles from his secondary vocal cords echoing only a little down the tunnels. Illuminating the space in a way that filled Sauraxen's heart. Enough sound waves to not only clarify his presence, but Dimae's too.

"Most IPA planets pick a second IPA language to learn as standard," Sauraxen explained.

"Mine was axelaxis," Basti interjected.

"Same," Matter said.

"I thought yours was ECE."

"Nei, I learnt ECE to communicate with Jonesy. And you."

"Anyway," Sauraxen interrupted. "ECE has a similar sound style to wrexi, even if we use different parts of our mouths to make the words."

"That's fascinating. I never considered prioritising a language based on noise-familiarity rather than grammatical-familiarity," Brruuh enthused.

Sauraxen tipped her chin up, beaming at her paramour. This was exactly why vava would love him. His enthusiasm, his joy, all those same things that Sauraxen had fallen in love with. But, as the welcoming party peered up and up and up at the pair of harrushetti, the tips of their ears brushing the ceiling above, Sauraxen very abruptly remembered that these assorted people might be her family, but to wrexi, they were predators only.

"We will escort you into the current homestead," one of the welcoming party said in ECE.

"Current?" Dimae asked.

"We're a nomadic people," Sauraxen explained. "The tunnels shift and change, so we move with them. Our homestead tends to move between the larger caverns, that's part of why we have a welcoming party, so they can lead us back to where they know the homestead to currently be. I'd be able to find it on my own, but it's easier with Xanaka."

"Thank you, Xanaka," Brruuh offered, pitching his voice low and smooth. A soothing tone.

The other wrexi suppressed a shudder.

Sauraxen's sensory hair wrapped around her, but she followed deeper into the tunnels and toward vava.

This was never going to have been easy, but Sauraxen had been away for long enough now to become used to the variety of aliens she would come into contact with in the course of her work and life in the wider IPA. These wrexi had either never left Pitzk, or they had returned for whatever reasons, and while Sauraxen may not have considered it, of course they would be put on edge by the assorted aliens she brought with her. Even Basti was predator enough to startle a wrexi.

Pitzk
Day 1

The top of the tunnel dipped, pressing Brruuh's ears to his head. He ducked, bending with the uneven stone surface as he trailed after the trio of wrexi and his crew. He and Matter had taken up the last two places on this convoy. Had Matter decided to bring up the rear for some specific purpose? Were ouaeahhn particularly sulphur resistant? Brruuh had picked to go as far back as possible to delay the inevitable. One person extra between him and meeting Sauraxen's vava.

Maybe Matter was avoiding the same thing.

In front of him Sauraxen and Basti were talking about how wrexi need for portability had encouraged some of the technological advancements in IPA standardisation. After all, as nomadic people, they tried to take everything with them just like a ship did but with only space enough for what they could carry. Brruuh kept half an ear on the conversation, the rest of his focus divided between figuring out where the tunnel walls were in the dim light or pitch darkness, and trying not to stress too hard about meeting Sauraxen's vava.

When the tunnel dipped further, Brruuh dropped to four legs. It stretched muscles that weren't used to being used; he hadn't done this since he was a kitten. There was no need on IPA ships or stations—at least not for a cognitivist.

"Oh, nei way!" Matter called from behind him. "You can swap between number of limbs?"

"I always have four limbs."

Matter laughed. "Okay, I phrased that badly."

"Can you not use your hands as feet?"

"Nei. Ouaeahhn were never quadrupedal, we evolved from trees. And humans can't really do it because of the way their—our?—knees point. Or, I suppose the primary leg joint being the knee rather than the ankle like yours."

"Big nerd!" Sauraxen called back from the front of

the group.

"Shut up, lizard who can bend her joints any which way is most convenient at the time like she doesn't even have bones," Matter called back.

It should have triggered Brruuh's protective instincts, registered as someone attacking the person with whom he was building a bond. And if he and his instincts could register it as the teasing it was, it should have pressed on that early and sensitive bond that the two were so close. It should have sparked jealousy. But he also shouldn't have been comfortable cuddling up in Sauraxen's bed with the addition of Matter and watching vids.

But it was Matter. Sauraxen had been very upfront in their initial conversations about not giving up her existing closeness with Matter. That had to be it. What other explanation was there?

The tunnels ran deep into the planet, leading the group through areas so warm, Brruuh had to pant to regulate his temperature and into ones so cold they felt like the very surface of Harrush. Sometimes the ceilings were tall enough that they stretched above Brruuh's head, other times they were so low he had to slide on his stomach to get through. At times the group stood two or three abreast, and sometimes it was so narrow Brruuh had to turn sideways to fit through the gap at all.

The path had begun to wear on him, his heart pounding in his chest and muscles aching from exertion. Ahead, Basti's breath came in short pants the way humans did with exertion—it still made Brruuh think of kittens, no matter how many times he was exposed to it. Behind him, Matter's breath hissed and the sound of their scuffing footsteps abruptly ceased.

Brruuh turned his head, but in the gloom of this tunnel, even his harrushetti eyes couldn't make them out.

Ahead of him, the rest of the group turned a corner, leaving him and Matter alone in the dark. Were they going to get lost here? Left abandoned just like he had been on the icy surface of Harrush? But he had to risk it, couldn't bear the thought of leaving Matter behind alone. Better to be in a pair.

"Are you okay?" he whispered.

"Crawling around is..." the pause held more words than any actual words could have. Avoidance. Textbook Matter from their very first meeting when they had tried needling him, pushing to the point they had needed to offer an apology for unintended upset. Even their suggestion that one of the dangers of space was the potential of being eaten by space whales. That avoidance popped up a lot. A barrier Matter had wrapped themself in that Brruuh really wanted to be able to help dismantle. If they would let him. But first he would have to bring it up.

"Are you—" stuck "—trapped?"

"I can keep going. I just need..." they trailed off again, strain all too evident in their voice.

The footsteps of the others had long since disappeared. They were alone here together. "Can is not the equivalent of—" should. Curse ECE and its abundance of words starting with S. How was Brruuh meant to communicate in a fraught situation like this while avoiding a letter he couldn't pronounce? "Is there any way I can assist?"

"You offering to carry me?" Matter teased.

"Would it help?"

The silence fell so deep Brruuh almost couldn't tell Matter was still there. Brruuh swallowed and inhaled long and slow, picking out the pieces of recognisable scent. Salt sting of Sebastian's sweat, that rich smokiness of a YaPar harrushetti, the coffee undercurrent of every member of Galactic Whale crew, and the engine scent that had buried itself beneath Sauraxen's scales. It didn't matter how many wrexi had passed through this way, how often, or how recent, Brruuh could scent his Ahthae.

Matter's scent was the strongest, their proximity making all the difference. It had shifted again, the way only Matter's scent seemed to do. A sharp spice of pain hovering around them, and the tempting whisper of eenya and home below it.

"You told me yourself that we are Ahthae."

"I did say that." Their voice was soft, hesitant.

"You brought me back from death, you and Axen together. Did you think I hadn't noticed the whale?" The whale he had made for Matter's birthday had ended up in his hospital bed. He hadn't seen it since returning to the ship.

"I guess I didn't think about it." They sighed. "It's not just about whether it would be appropriate for you or not."

"It would be," he reassured. "But what else?"

"Accepting help isn't…"

"Easy?"

"Put simply."

"You don't want to need it?"

"I feel like I shouldn't. Not from you."

Brruuh's ears twitched hard enough to brush against the roof of the low tunnel. "Me particularly?"

"You nearly died recently."

"Thus I s-tshould leave you here in this tunnel?"

"I'm not stuck."

Brruuh huffed his disbelief. If they weren't stuck, they wouldn't have stopped. "I'm going to touch you now."

"Brruuh—" They cut off as Brruuh wrapped his hands carefully around their upper arms and dragged them onto his back. The tiniest, suppressed pained noise escaped them as their breathing turned sharp.

Brruuh pressed himself low to the ground, stomach brushing the stone below.

Matter rested their cheek between his shoulder blades, arms wrapped loosely around his chest. His heart smashed against his ribs like a prisoner in a cage, desperate to escape. They must be able to feel it;

surely it was pounding against them just as strong.

It wasn't acceptable on Harrush to share this kind of contact, this level of contact with someone other than a Bond Mate. Not even family would press against each other this tightly.

But this was Matter, so the rules were different. Matter was ouaeahhn-human. Matter had claimed him as Ahthae, more and different than family. Matter was his almost Bond Mate's best friend. This was a medical emergency. Surely this situation was different.

If only his body and emotions could catch up with his logic.

If only it didn't feel like more than necessity.

Sauraxen's scent was easy to follow, even beneath the sulphur distortion it stood out like a cleanly painted arrow beneath him. Especially with the overlay of the rest of the crew.

"I'm sorry," Matter whispered.

"Nei apologies," Brruuh whispered back.

"Thank you."

Brruuh swallowed thickly and tried to ignore the way those words had his heart thundering even more violently.

After a long while, they emerged into a large chamber, all the same smooth rock as the tunnels but illuminated by the glowing mushrooms Sauraxen had cultivated in the engineering bay. Wrexi filled the space, sitting and standing and lying around in small clusters of bright silver-blue. Their soft chittering deafened him in the wake of the tunnel-silence—where only his and Matter's breathing had carried.

Brruuh stood slowly, letting Matter find their feet as his eyes flicked over groups of wrexi, searching for those out of place. Some wrexi held smaller ones—hatchlings—to their chests, obviously also raising parents. Most had small bags at their hips, a strap stretching over their shoulder another around their waist. In one cluster, every wrexi had a datapad on their lap, leaning to point and poke at each other's.

And across the cavern, the other harrushetti stood painfully tall compared to everyone else. There was a larger gap between that cluster than the others. Space placed between outsiders and the community.

He glanced at Matter again and started over to the group.

Sebastian

The ill-health of Sauraxen's vava wasn't evident in any way Basti could perceive. Xe looked so much like Sauraxen. Not that Basti was all that familiar with wrexi as a whole; would he be able to pick out the markers of difference? Still, the way Sauraxen spoke, the way she held herself, it all matched with her vava as xe greeted them. "It's so nice to meet my hatchling's chosen companions! Let me guess..." Xe gestured to Basti with a hand. "You're boxers-lamp Basti?"

Basti groaned, clapping a hand over his face. "I thought I had lived that down."

"I'm afraid that is the kind of thing you never get to live down."

"Boxers-lamp?" Dimae asked.

"You know Sauraxen and I met when we got put as roommates for our Master's Degrees?"

Dimae nodded.

"Well, Sauraxen had gone away for a few days, a local space station internship. And I took advantage of the privacy." Sharing a room was beneficial: cheaper than solo dorms, chance of built-in friendship, and even left a chance of not being assigned a roommate at all and getting a double room for half the price. It also meant minimal privacy as you shared space with a relative stranger whose bed was only a short distance from yours. "The person I shared that time with couldn't find his boxers when he went to leave. So he just left without them. Sauraxen found them when she got back."

"On the lamp," Sauraxen finished.

"On the lamp," Basti confirmed.

Dimae tucked his face into Basti's shoulder to snicker.

"You would be the doctor, Dimae?" Sauraxen's

vava asked.

"Correct."

"Matter, of course," Sauraxen's vava cheered as Matter and Brruuh joined the group.

Matter tipped their head back in a wrexi smile. "It's so good to finally meet you!"

Sauraxen's vava wrapped xyr arms and sensory hair around Matter in an all-enveloping hug.

Dimae stepped back and trilled a question at Brruuh, who beeped back a response and flicked an ear in obvious dismissal.

"Claustrophobia?" Dimae hissed in ECE, disbelieving.

"Ja," Brruuh snapped back, flicking his ear again. "From the death of my family. Leave it."

Dimae huffed but Basti laid a hand on his arm. This wasn't a conversation for here and now, whatever it had started with.

"You have to tell me the name she chose," Sauraxen's vava insisted, barely letting go of Matter.

"What do you mean?" Matter asked.

"Wrexi have childhood names that we grow out of," Sauraxen explained. "We are our vava's little ones: Sau and Raxen."

"You mean to tell me we've been nicknaming you 'little one' this whole time?"

"Ja. Or just 'little' Axen is more like 'little'. It's a complicated language."

"They all are," Brruuh murmured.

"I don't know this one from the stories," Sau interrupted. "My raxen, why have you not told me about this one?"

Sauraxen twisted her hands together. "Vava, this is Brruuh, my…"

Sau's head tilted back, exposing xyr entire neck. Xe let out a series of peeps that could very well have been a laugh. "You and your fickle star-bound heart."

"It's not fickle!" Sauraxen argued, voice petulant. "That's the whole point."

"What happened to Liz?"

"She…" Sauraxen shifted into the wrexi language, conversing quickly with her vava. No doubt explaining the breakup that had taken place before she joined Basti's crew.

Basti took the moment to look over at Matter, watching the conversation as if they understood. Did they speak Wrexi now?

Sau turned to Brruuh, opening xyr arms to embrace him the same way xe had Matter. Basti opened his mouth to interrupt, to explain that a harrushetti wouldn't appreciate such a welcome but Brruuh stepped into the contact and let out an explosive purr.

"Welcome to the family," Sau said. "That's what you lot do, isn't it? Join families?"

"It is," Brruuh confirmed.

"I didn't think I'd get another axen at this age, I'm glad to be proven wrong."

Matter

Once the wrexi around them had got a little more used to the presence of outsiders, strangers and predators all, they had started sharing food around. Matter wasn't entirely sure what it was they had put together, but Dimae sniffed each bowl before Basti could try it to ensure there were no bugs within. "It's really not a big deal," Basti had tried to argue. "It's only a mild allergy."

"You can play—what is ECE phrase?—quick and losing with your allergies when we have easy access to medi-centres," Dimae argued. "Not in the tunnels of Pitzk."

"Fast and loose," Basti had corrected, but accepted the argument as it stood.

Once the food was done with, someone had struck up a beat, followed by a melody and wrexi pulled together to dance and sing and celebrate the return of a star-bound one.

Matter let Sauraxen pull them into the group, joining the dance and letting the music and the crowd fuel their body and its movements. Settling into the movements of the crowd, Matter's personal shields lowered, filling them with the joy of shared experience. The bonds forged in a crowd of dancers mending pieces of them just like meaningful contact.

Breath ghosted their neck and a whisper of, "Come with me," tickled their ear.

Matter let the wrexi guide them from the crowd to a smaller tunnel secluded by a pile of rocks. "I just want to ask," the wrexi said, hand still in Matter's hand. "The large humming predator, he carried you out of the tunnel like a hatchling…?"

Child-coded by a wrexi. Wonderful.

"I said that wrong. Are you—"

"I'm an adult," Matter cut in.

"Definitely said it wrong. I meant are you with him? And are you well?"

"Brruuh is just a friend—" Better not to get into the concept of Ahthae here and now. "And I'm disabled, but I'm fine. I just couldn't tunnel."

"Oh, good, because I—I'm Lacha."

"Matter."

"Like the stuff that makes up space?"

Matter laughed. "Unintended coincidence. It's the middle portion of my full name."

"Oh?"

"Ymmattrahni."

"Ee-matt-ra-ah-ni?" The syllables didn't quite come out right, but the sound all pressed together well enough.

"Pretty much."

"It's pretty, can I call you that?"

"If you like."

"Reluctance?"

"Most people don't."

"I'm not most people. I'm Lacha."

Matter smiled, then realised it wouldn't translate and tipped their chin back in the wrexi version.

"Do you know the wrexi custom for disappearing behind rocks?"

"Nei."

"It's for…" Lacha trailed off, searching for a word and pressing hands and fingers together in a complicated weave.

"Coupling?" Matter suggested.

"I like how you move. I was hoping to get the more focused version. If you're amenable? Able?"

Sauraxen always said she was an outlier when it came to wrexi, most didn't go for relationships. The custom was to couple as you desired in pairs or groups, and only raising parents had any instinct toward hatchlings when they eventually broke free of their eggs. And it wasn't like Matter was unfamiliar with how Matter-shaped beings and wrexi-shaped beings could find pleasure together. "I am both amenable and able. I should warn you, though, I'm… Can I take your hand?"

Lacha offered it.

Matter pressed it between their own, concentrating hard on sharing just through that point of contact.

On a planet like this, naturally so hostile, the people grew hardy, sturdy against the dangers that surrounded them. They couldn't be in tune like ouaeahhn, couldn't risk the discordant melody of emotion. Yet, still, they needed to be able to move and flee from danger as a unit, so some emotive connection must exist.

Matter's internal shields were strong; enough years off Ouaeahhn would do that. And the pieces of them that were more human helped build upon that base, especially with people they hadn't yet come to know. But if they really concentrated…

Lacha gasped, fingers gripping tight to Matter, sharps claws digging into their skin. Tiny pinpricks that blossomed out into what Matter recognise even before it grew into a new pattern. Ounu, a formative moment, something they would never forget even if it hadn't etched itself into their skin.

Lacha pressed a hand to Matter's cheek, letting out a soft string of chirps that Matter might have been able to translate if they weren't quite so fast. Still, where their skin touched scales, emotion warmed them: compassion, care, love.

The feedback looped, opening Matter up more than they intended. They tried to yank their hand back but Lacha held fast. "Trust me with it," they whispered. "If the sulphur does not kill you, what can?"

"Idiom?" Matter asked.

Lacha nodded. "You and I are strong enough to share this."

Matter pressed their forehead against Lacha's. The wrexi nuzzled closer.

"How do I get the cloth off?" Lacha asked.

Matter reached for their zip.

"Let me."

Matter let Lacha tug off their jumpsuit, kissed down the pattern of blue and purple that swirled down Lacha's scales as Lacha trailed fingers over the raised patterns across Matter's skin. Patterns of a life well lived, a universe explored, bonds forged and trusts broken.

Their shoulder came down a little heavy on the hard ground beneath, pain still lingering from crashing into Sauraxen's door brought to shocking light once more. They yelped. Lacha paused, hands reaching to soothe.

"I'm okay," Matter reassured.

"Tunnels?" Lacha asked.

"Before, I fell into a door."

"Door?"

"Temporary wall."

Lacha giggled, swinging a leg to straddle Matter's bare lap—when had the jumpsuit come all the way off? Where were their boots?

Matter leaned up to meet their mouth in a kiss. Letting Lacha guide them more gently back down and roaming their own hands across the foreign yet familiar feeling of scales, lingering where Lacha let out pleased sounds.

The opened tele-empathic bond between them swirled, like emotions drawn into a gravity well. Pain: the pricks of scales, the lingering endless ache of joints long since beyond repair, the huffing rattle of sulphur in lungs. Pleasure: of the dance, of being seen, of shared touch. Nerves of meeting someone new. Fear that lingered over everything wrexi did, and specifically for Sau's wellbeing. And that beautiful thing that Matter had only ever been able to describe as connection, the way bonding with someone would light them up from the inside. All of it combined and fed off itself, off each of them, until the pleasure crested together, leaving Lacha and Matter cuddled in the aftermath.

"You're an outsider, do you want to sleep here with me?"

"Is that too weird? I can deal if it's time to separate," Matter offered.

Lacha shrugged. "What's the point of being with an outsider if I don't get to be weird?"

Matter laughed quietly. "Let's stay here for a while then."

Pitzk

Day 2

Sauraxen

She'd been off planet too long. Got too used to the human way of doing things, the IPA way of doing things. Because, despite the way her vava had so lovingly welcomed everyone, and despite the revelry of the previous night, all Sauraxen wanted was to have a private conversation with her vava. But privacy wasn't a thing on Pitzk. There were no doors to close, no real way to signal wanting everyone else to keep their distance from a conversation.

And vava was currently sat with Brruuh, chatting with one another in that happy animated way vava always seemed to do. Building bonds easily.

"How are you feeling?" Sauraxen asked xem in a whisper.

Sau tilted xyr head, offering a platitude that did nothing to reassure Sauraxen. Xe opened xyr arms and Sauraxen dove into them, snuggling close like she was a hatchling all over again.

"I'm sorry I had to call you like that," xe murmured in their shared home tongue.

Sauraxen didn't respond. What could she say? She hated it too? She wished vava could get better? That she had broken a plethora of IPA regulations to get here in time? That she was enraged that none of Sau's other hatchlings seemed to care that they were about to lose xem?

Did it matter less to those on Pitzk? Had they already made their peace with it? Was Sauraxen somehow less wrexi? Less grown up?

"Tell me about your cognitivist," Sau invited, glancing at Brruuh, who had shifted his attention to the wider cavern, leaning back against the wall behind him in a relaxed posture and easily accepting that this was a private conversation.

"He's wonderful," Sauraxen replied. "And so weird!"

"Tell me," Sau enthused.

So Sauraxen started on the story of how she and Brruuh met, how he had seemed so scary at first and how she had quickly come to realise he was nothing like the predator's air he gave off. How he had stumbled over his words trying to confess his feelings, how harrushetti had hyper-monogamy, and how he was still so kind to Matter, even though less serious partners she'd had in the past were jealous or snippy. Things she'd shared already in her letters to home but different because this time they were together.

All the while, Sau trailed hands over her sensory hair. Xe asked relevant questions and laughed or gasped or joked in the right places, using what messages xe'd got from Sauraxen's time on the Galactic Whale and other times she'd spent with Basti and Matter outside that.

At some point, as they shifted from Brruuh-focused to wider crew stories, they swapped into ECE and invited Brruuh back into the conversation. At another point Basti and Dimae came over to settle around them, sharing their own perspectives of their stories and launching into more. Leaning against one another in ways that most matched their cultural expectations: Basti against Dimae, Brruuh settling himself half against Sauraxen, pressing her between him and her vava in a delightful way.

Matter, social butterfly type that they were, had been spending time amongst the other wrexi, learning skills and making contact. They appeared every now and again in the edge of Sauraxen's perception, but it wasn't until the evening that they came to settle with more luminance on their reflective skin than before. Glowing yellow and blue like the mushrooms. They settled themself between Brruuh and Basti, opposite Sauraxen in the circle they'd formed together.

"And that was when Matter began chasing me around the room with the whale," Brruuh finished.

Vava laughed, shoulders shaking underneath Sauraxen.

"Hey!" Matter protested. "It wasn't me, it was the whale. He wanted your bone marrow." They made the same slurping noise they had chased Brruuh with, sending him pressing into Sauraxen and making vava laugh so hard xe started to cough.

Across their little circle, Dimae stiffened in that way that made her think predator. His ears flicked back in a harrushetti grimace.

Sau waved off any concern. "Did the whale succeed?"

Brruuh rumbled a negative.

"He used me as a shield," Sauraxen added.

Sau laughed again even as Brruuh protested.

Dimae

The breath of a thousand wrexi tickled the sensitive hair inside Dimae's ears. Their twitching and shuffling felt like it was rubbing his fur raw. Even Sebastian's soft snores next to him didn't soothe like they normally did. Sleeping in a huge cavern, exposed to everyone else was beyond strange.

With a huff, Dimae shifted away from his little sleeping group. He shuffled quietly over to an alcove that seemed to be the perfect seat; it even had a convenient cluster of those bioluminescent mushrooms growing out of the top of it like a personal lamp. A weak and dim personal lamp but still.

When Dimae had first left Harrush, he had known to expect things to be weird and alien. But, even on EC.623, when he had visited Basti's family for the first time and had his first experience of rain, so much of the world matched his experience only a little askew. The same shape but a different colour. Like Brruuh's YaBin stripes to his YaPar rosettes. But here on Pitzk...

Worse still, he had known it was going to be alien and he was still struggling with just how alien it was. Harrushetti were a key member of the IPA council, where wrexi hardly ever left Pitzk. Of course his life in the IPA looked more like Harrush than here. It had been, still was, shaped by people like Dimae. He had never even considered if others would have the same experience.

He pulled his datapad from the small pouch on his belt. Surprised at the lack of connection to IPA databases despite having known in advance he wouldn't have it. The only other place he'd been so out of touch had been the Chluian retreat, and that had only been inside the building.

Sebastian rolled onto his back, arms and legs flung out every which way and mouth fully open. Dimae huffed a subdued laugh. Trust his Bond Mate.

Beside him, Brruuh curled around Sauraxen, one arm slung across her waist. Together. That was a concept. Predator and prey. But Brruuh might die of heartbreak if it didn't work so… Who knew? It wasn't like Dimae could condemn someone for finding bonds outside their own planet and culture.

Sauraxen's hand clutched at her vava. And Matter, a short distance away, lay on their own. They'd been notably absent from the little group ever since the first night when they had disappeared into the crowd of dancing wrexi.

Dimae's ears flattened against his head. With the way their skin shimmered in wrexi blue, silver, yellow, and purple, it wasn't hard to tell that they had been finding meaningful contact here. He tried to quash his own cultural expectations. Matter wasn't harrushetti, they didn't have to abide by harrushetti customs. They *needed* meaningful contact to survive.

But how meaningful could this possibly be?

He shook himself, focusing on the datapad in front of him, dragging research files and notes out of their respective folders so he could flick easily between them. Whether he'd be able to do anything about Sau's illness was yet to be ascertained. Nobody had technically asked him to try. It seemed wrexi had long since given up on the idea of healing this particular illness, but harrushetti medicine was the best in the IPA, so he might as well look into it. He couldn't just do nothing and watch this welcoming and kind wrexi die without even trying to fix it. Or make it easier. Give more time, or better time.

Plus, it would cover their tracks if they got pulled in by the IPA. Notes and investigations, documentation of this illness and its effects would only help their case. And research was old hat at this point, all too easy to go through the motions of highlighting important sections, feeding them into a master doc of notes of his own that seamlessly morphed into a research paper he could present for a grant or a trial or even just access the relevant medicines if there were any.

Not that his notes thus far made much sense. The sulphur-yellow tint to Sau's scales might mean nothing, might just be part of aging for wrexi, but there was no harm noting it down. The cough was the most obvious symptom. But Dimae had noticed too, how Sau passed over food, reluctant to take down much. He'd noticed Sau needing to sit more, the way xe moved more stiffly. So much of what he observed in Matter mid-flare present here too.

He flicked between notes and research papers. He hadn't found much on wrexi within IPA databases. Wished he could have reached out to his lizardoid-expert colleague for advice.

A rasping gasp drew him from the depths of his research, a double claw-scratch of new notes completed. By the time his eyes had adjusted from the light of his datapad to the dimness of the surrounding chamber, Matter was sat up with their hands pressed to their eyes, breathing with intentional slowness.

Dimae cleared his throat, an exceedingly human announcement of his presence.

Matter jerked to look at him. "Can't sleep either?"

Why did they have to be so casual in the wake of something so obviously distressing? "Ja," he said. "It's too busy in here, messes with my ears."

Matter smiled sadly. "It's quieter than Ouaeahhn. Everybody is in everybody else's heads there."

"That would be a lot."

"It is. Probably not so much for you, what with your natural shielding and all."

"Or it would be the niggling, ear-twitching feeling that there is a thing happening that you cannot access."

Matter grimaced. "That does sound worse." They shifted toward him, scooting on their butt like a human toddler. "What are you up to?"

"Researching Sau's illness."

"You can get signal on Pitzk? I thought they had to get to a broadcasting tower to ping messages off the orbiting IPA satellite."

"Medical pads have research tools built in." He turned the datapad to show Matter the wider edge where the extra data storage sat. "I have a large database to pull from, but not the entire thing."

"Snazzy."

"I don't know that word."

"Colloquialism, it means fancy in a fun way."

"Medical research is fun," Dimae mused.

Matter laughed.

Dimae's ears twitched. Were they laughing at his enjoyment?

"Oh, I've upset you. I didn't mean…" They sighed. "What did I do?"

"Misinterpretation, I think," Dimae allowed. "You were laughing at me."

"Nei. It was shaa tsea."

"That's Ouaeahhn?"

"Ja." They let out a breath that tickled over Dimae's fur as they tried to translate it. "Surprised joy—that's a bad translation but it's the best I could think of."

"You were laughing not out of humour, but enjoyment?"

"Exactly. I was surprised that you like medical research, and then enjoying that it's something someone could enjoy. I've always had horrible experience with medicine; I forget that's not how it is for everyone."

"Being in a medical crisis is always bad," Dimae said slowly, choosing his words with care. "It doesn't matter how well it goes, doesn't matter how good or kind your medical officers are, the fact of having needed the care makes it a bad experience."

He hadn't known that before. Had thought there was something he could do to leave patients untraumatised by their medical crises. Now he knew better. His duty as a medical officer in a situation like that was to minimise the trauma. To do everything he could to get the person better while respecting their wants. To ease the difficulty of it was not the same as making it easy, but it almost mattered more.

It was a piece of the puzzle cognitivists had been rumbling about for years and Dimae, like a fool, had largely dismissed it. Ego large enough to believe he was better than the other doctors they were talking about. He had believed the system that listed body and mind as two separate pieces, as if his ability to die of heartbreak, or Matter's need for meaningful contact didn't fly in the face of such theories.

Beside him Matter suppressed a yawn.

"Try to get more rest?" Dimae suggested.

"Can't."

Dimae's eyes flicked over them, assessing for pain, assessing for medical intervention. But maybe this was another mind-body situation. Maybe it was the same problem Dimae kept finding himself in. "Dreams?"

Matter nodded.

Dimae scooted over in his alcove, making space for Matter to take up. They settled in next to him as he turned back to his research. "I'm here if you need anything," he offered.

Matter hummed.

Another claw-scratch of notes and Matter's head landed softly on Dimae's shoulder. Instinct yelled at him to move it, to push them off. But he glanced down to see their chest moving with even, slow breaths.

He sighed and turned back to his notes.

Pitzk
Day 3

Sebastian

Basti's back ached in a way it wouldn't have twenty years ago if he'd slept on a hard stone floor for a few days. He stood up, suppressing a groan and tried twisting his body this way and that to stretch out the pain.

"You okay?" Matter asked, placing a hand on the wrexi by their side with whom they had been talking. Like they were pausing the conversation to swap focus to Basti.

"Feeling my age," Basti complained as his back crackled and popped.

"Big birthday soon," they teased, their breath disrupting the steam over the small bowl they clutched in their free hand and sending the rich scent toward Basti.

"Is that coffee?"

"Something like it."

Basti reached out to steal the bowl from Matter but they jerked away with a snorted giggle.

"Get your own!"

"What's a birthday?" the wrexi at Matter's side asked. They were paler than Sauraxen, with delicate blue and purple swirls painted down their side—or were those naturally occurring patterns?—that went all the way to the tip of their fingers cupped around a similar shallow bowl to Matter's. The pair sat close together, legs crossed under them and knees in contact. Matter's hand remained where it was on the wrexi's forearm.

"It's an annual celebration of the day you... hatched," Matter explained.

"We don't hatch exactly," Basti clarified.

"Is that necessary context right now?" Matter asked.

"Like a naming ceremony but every year?" the wrexi asked.

"I think so," Matter agreed even as Basti asked, "What's a naming ceremony?"

"When we're young," the wrexi explained, "We are known as our vava's little ones."

Sau and Sauraxen had explained that when they first arrived in the wrexi homestead. Basti made another valiant attempt for Matter's not-coffee. Matter slapped lightly at his hands with the hand that had been resting on the wrexi.

The wrexi suppressed a laugh as they continued to explain. "When I was a hatchling, I was Xanakaxen until I chose Lacha. It's a celebration of choosing maturity, you feel ready to choose a name and become an adult. We go to this huge ceremonial chamber and eat mushrooms, it's a good time."

"It sounds it," Matter confirmed.

"Sauraxen left before hers," Lacha continued. "That's why she's still an axen."

Basti nodded slowly. "I'm gonna go get not-coffee."

Matter tilted their chin up in a wrexi smile and shifted back into their conversation with Lacha, speaking in slow and stilted Wrexi pips and squeaks.

Basti left them to it and trailed his way across the room toward Sauraxen. She was also speaking in Wrexi, this conversation rapid enough to wash over Basti in that unintelligible way unknown languages always did. Sauraxen was angry with the other wrexi, though. The sharp shift of her hands made that more than clear.

Sauraxen spun, coming face to chest with Basti. She tilted her head up to him and then back into a wrexi smile. "Basti, you're awake! Finally."

Basti gasped mockingly. "Are you picking on me, Sauraxen of Pitzk?"

"Would I do that, Sleepy Sebastian Jones of EC.623?" The tease was one he'd heard before. A common back and forth they had bounced off each other from the start of their burgeoning friendship when Sauraxen realised how long Sebastian—and other humans—needed to sleep compared to wrexi.

The wrexi Sauraxen had been arguing with muttered something. Sauraxen's sensory hair lifted.

"Matter has a coffee-like substance," Basti accused, maintaining his teasing tone.

"Let's get you some," Sauraxen said, leading Basti away from the arguing wrexi and across the cavern.

"Can I ask what the argument was about?" he asked.

"Ratch is... He was also raised by Sau and I was asking why he wasn't more concerned, why he wasn't offering care for xem. But he's not a vava, so care isn't easy to..." She shook herself. "And then he accused me of being too alien and being too young to understand."

"That sucks," Basti offered. "I get the alien thing sometimes, on terraforming day and stuff. Family and neighbours have very human mannerisms and I've spent most of my life fitting in with aliens, with Dimae. We all take on our" —what was the word Matter always used?—"Ahthae's qualities. It's normal."

"I think I'm more annoyed by the childification."

"Do you think part of it is that you're still an axen?"

Sauraxen tilted her head, serving Basti a bowl of not-coffee.

"Matter's friend," he gestured to Lacha now with forehead pressed against Matter's, "Said something about you not getting to do your big birthday thing."

"The IPA transport turned up early, we had to cancel it."

"What if you did that? I'm sure Sau would appreciate one more celebration too."

Sauraxen

The central chamber hadn't changed since Sauraxen has last been here, watching Lacha choose their name. The central rocky outcropping overflowed with bioluminescent mushrooms, lighting the space almost too bright for wrexi eyes to cope with. Thus the reason it was a ceremonial space despite having a surplus of foodstuff growing in it. When she had first come here as a tiny hatchling, she had tucked her face into her vava's neck, the light too bright for her young eyes. Now she stood, freshly scale-scrubbed and painted, as the wrexi around her hissed at the brightness. This was nothing compared to an IPA Station, barely as bright as the standard lighting on Galactic Whale, a system that had been painstakingly shifted one way and the other to optimise it for all the species aboard.

"Young one," her vava called in Wrexi from the fountain of mushrooms. Xe had disappeared rapidly after Sauraxen had enquired about Basti's plan. The elders and her vava setting up what needed to be organised as Lacha, Xanaka, and a few others had led Sauraxen off to get cleaned up. Notably Ratch hadn't participated in that.

The wrexi elders, with sensory hair turning dark at the tips, clustered behind Sau, blocking a little of the mushroom light from behind the pedestal below a stalactite that dripped a slow and even measure, like the heartbeat of the world.

Sauraxen approached her vava's open arms, taking xyr hands in hers and letting xem help her step over the mushrooms surrounding the pedestal without disturbing them.

"Today you claim your name," vava said. "And, with it, your adulthood and freedom."

"My adulthood and freedom are well established," Sauraxen muttered.

"It's the traditional words," one of the elders chastised.

"My star-bound one, returned to celebrate with

her family," Sau amended, switching briefly to ECE and tilting xyr head toward the crew of the Galactic Whale, loitering together at the edge of the cavern. "Returned with her truest sense of self to share with us all. An adulthood established in the mysteries of the night sky and brought home for a family never forgotten." Xe switched back to wrexi, "What name have you chosen?"

Sauraxen took a deep breath, filling her lungs with the scent of caverns and mushrooms, wrexi tinged with the undercurrent of sulphur. What name had she chosen? She should probably have given this more thought while she was getting ready for the ceremony to take place. When she was younger, she had been so focused on learning about engineering, so focused on getting good enough to be accepted into IPA training. Even amongst the stars, surrounded by aliens, she'd left Sauraxen as her name as a reminder of her home, her origins.

Basti had a family name. Brruuh and Dimae both had family-clan names. Of her current crew, only Matter was surname free, another person who ended up with 'of planet' filling that IPA box.

Her crew's breath, so different from the way wrexi breathed in a way that remained completely impossible to explain, lingered on the edge of her consciousness, travelling into the uneven surfaces of the cavern, making each ridge of each mushroom clear to her sensory vision. She was, unbreakably bonded to these aliens just as she was to her vava. She had built adult bonds with them, had considered herself an adult ever since leaving the planet. And they had always known her by a singular name. Had nicknamed her by it.

"I choose Sauraxen," she said finally.

"You can't do that!" Ratch called from somewhere in the crowd. "You'll forever be confused with Sau's hatchlings."

"I don't even live here, Ratch!" Sauraxen snapped back. "Plus, is vava is dying of the wasting anyway, xe isn't going to be raising any more hatchlings. And I'm not a vava, so I wouldn't be raising Sauraxenaxens."

Ratch's head tucked down. "I still think it should be up to the Elders."

"Well?" Sau asked the elders.

They huddled together, scales less reflective than the younger ones. Heads moving with their muted peeps and suppressed pips. A pang of grief stung Sauraxen at the knowledge her vava would never look like that, would never get to become an elder. Would never be—"Your logic?" one elder demanded.

"I have been an adult under this name for many years. My Ahthae know me with this name—"

"Ahthae?"

"It's an ouaeahhn word, it means the family-we. It's the people you've built bonds with, more than friendship, more like a family you've built together."

"Continue," the elder invited.

"Sauraxen is the name I used when I forged those bonds. The name I am known by in IPA space. I am Sauraxen the engineer, Sauraxen of Pitzk. Celebrating my vava in my name is part of where I am from and my name will always call back to that. I want to keep it."

The elders conferred again. "We do not see flaw in the young one's logic. One's first adult name does not need to last the rest of their adult life. Should she wish to return to Pitzk, she is welcome, also, to take a planetary name in addition."

"My little one," Sau sighed lovingly. "I grant you your adult name of choice. Sauraxen will become Sauraxen, Engineer of Pitzk." Xe gestured for Sauraxen to pick a mushroom from the pedestal.

She leaned into the collection, gently plucking one that shone an odd purple-grey. A rare and special mushroom compared to the blue and yellow ones that filled most of the tunnels. The purple-grey ones were harder to grow, less hardy, often overlooked.

She chewed it, letting the flavour play over her tongue. Unlike any flavour she was previously familiar with. She'd been too young to try such a rare thing before she left.

"Wow." Brruuh's unmistakeable rasp.

"Look at her shine," Matter agreed in a whisper spiked with wonder.

Quake

Brruuh

The ceremony was hardly over, Sauraxen still glowing as she helped her vava and the elders off the platform, wrexi just beginning to swarm her with affection. Brruuh was in the process of deciding whether to squeeze through the crowd and sweep her into his arms, or whether to wait for her to make it to him when the world started shaking around him.

Brruuh's ears clamped down against his head. A thunderous rumble echoed through the cave systems. His heart stuttered, seeming to stop. He was going to die this time. There was no way to escape twice.

Instead of the dark caves and luminous mushrooms with a cluster of wrexi, Brruuh's eyes played out scenes of snow and the inescapable blast of water as the world around him shattered. Icy cold floodwater swept around him, brushing up against his fur in a desperate wave. Trying to push him into the depths of it. He would sink there. Sink and try so desperately to keep his breath inside his body in an ultimately futile attempt to stay alive.

This was how he died. This time. Last time. Every time. Bodies of YaBin harrushetti far beyond saving swirling around him in a whirlpool, his family, his friends, his whole world. And all Brruuh had was the ability to cling to a close piece of alien tree with surprising buoyancy. How unfortunate not to have a tree this time. Then again, it would almost be worse to survive it this time. To lose everything once more. The ship he had settled into, the family he had built. His paramour. And, even if he could survive it, broken beyond repair this time. He would be unable to open himself up to the prospect of bonds only to have them ripped away.

Not that he could. He was in love now. If a harrushetti's Bond Mate died, so did the harrushetti. Shouldn't he have died of heartbreak last time, with the loss of everyone he had ever loved? But Brruuh had always been a little broken. Always been a little wrong.

Something tugged his wrist. He tried to fight it, but

it was insistent and surprisingly strong. Sounds, something like words, swirled against his ears underneath the rush of water. He couldn't hear it. Couldn't understand. But the thing smelled like family and like a tree, so he went. Instinct and memory leading more than thought.

The tugging led him into a large tunnel. The light disappeared around them, pitching them into blackness as dark as death. The grip didn't lessen, his guide barely slowing at all. The rumbling still pressing against their every side.

And then they were falling.

Dimae

"**B**asti!" Dimae had been swept off his feet in the wash of running wrexi. Between the shuffle of the thousand sets of feet and the continuing rumble and scrape of rocks against one another as the world around them collapsed and reformed, Dimae couldn't make anything out. He shouter louder. "Sebastian, where are you?"

"Dimae!" Sauraxen appeared, slithering up the tunnel wall, gripping her bare hands and feet to it in a way that made Dimae's brain hurt. His ears flicked to reassure him that he was, in fact, still stood the right way up. "You need to stop shouting," Sauraxen insisted. "Basti will be in one of the other tunnels—"

"I need to get to him!"

"I know. But you're panicking people. You need to calm down or we'll never be able to start looking for somewhere safe to reconvene. The longer you keep shouting, the longer you have to wait to find Basti."

"What do you mean?"

"This tunnel might give way. It's just a quake, they happen, we have a system but that system only works if you stop scaring people."

"I'm scared."

"I know that too. But the best way to get less scared is to get safe and make a plan."

It didn't help. How could it possibly help? What plan could solve this? He needed Basti, needed to know he was safe, needed to hold him in his arms and reassure himself with the softness of his warm skin, the steady thump of his heart, and the ticking regularity of his breath against Dimae's fur.

"Lacha is hurt," Sauraxen said. How was her voice so calm? "We need a capable medical officer. And I know you are one under all that panic."

That worked. Dimae had been in medicine far longer than he had known Basti. While pairing with a Bond Mate fundamentally changed who he was and how he behaved, Dimae wasn't giving up his life's calling. If he had fought his familial hierarchy to get into the medical field to begin with, he wasn't ruining his chance to help someone. He clamped down on the panicked growls and focused on Sauraxen. "Where is Lacha?"

"Keep moving with the wrexi for now and I'll get you to them."

With a stiff nod and well trained somewhat strained self-control, Dimae followed the river of wrexi through tunnels that grew and shrank, feeling like nothing so much as that human story of the little girl down the rabbit hole. Basti had read it to him while he was in recovery from the events of Clickclick. A disorientating tale that reminded Dimae of his first terraforming day on EC.623, where long held traditions were so familiar that everyone forgot to explain them and Dimae had spent most of his time bewildered, confused, and slightly on edge. Thinking about Basti sent a sharp pain through his abdomen but he ignored it. Basti wasn't dead until proven. That was all he could cling to.

The wrexi next to him jerked his head toward Dimae. Skittering away with obvious fear.

Dimae swallowed and clamped tighter to his self-control. No vocalisations. And no thinking about Basti.

Pitzk
Day 4

Matter

Matter's head ached something fierce. They forced their eyes open to peer around the darkness. Not even the tiniest peek of stars visible in whatever hole they'd managed to fall into this time. They sent out tele-empathic feeler, no ouaeahhn around, but another being was in this space with them. Someone with walls sturdy enough that Matter might as well have walked straight into a physical one. They groaned.

What had happened? Who was here? Oh, right, they'd been on Pitzk. The naming ceremony. And then... The world had started to shake and the wrexi had all bolted like a single unit, and Brruuh had gone all glassy-eyed and frozen.

It was good that they remembered, right? That was supposed to mean no concussion. Could Matter even get a concussion? Wasn't it a human-only thing? Weird question to ask Dimae when they next saw him: am I human enough for concussions?

"Brruuh?" they asked the creature in the dark. It had to be Brruuh, right? Because they'd grabbed him. He had frozen, lips pulled back just a little over sharp canines. Harrushetti weren't supposed to freeze. So Matter had grabbed him and started to run, trying to match the unit of wrexi, and then…

"Here," he wheezed.

Matter almost asked if he was okay, but that would be a stupid question. They didn't know much about the YaBin disaster, only what that one doctor on Harrush had told them, but what they did know painted a picture of Brruuh in the midst of post-situational trauma. Shame it wasn't the other way around, at least Brruuh would know what to do to help. "Are you hurt?"

"Nei."

"That's good."

"You?"

Always, but that wasn't a helpful response and it wouldn't get a laugh right now. "Just the usual amount, I think." It was always hard to tell.

"That's a bad answer."

"Honest, though."

"I'm actually a little more uncomfortable knowing you're distressed enough to be taking this professionally."

A shocked laugh escaped Matter. "Just because I'm being honest doesn't mean I'm being serious."

"That's okay then."

"Where are you? I can't see for shit in this darkness."

Brruuh's hand tapped at their arm and they grabbed hold of it in a loose grip. That helped. Knowing he was there was far different to feeling it physically.

"Do you think we should just wait here to get rescued?" Matter asked. "Or do we make a plan?"

"I'd feel better with a plan."

"Okay, cat-boy, what can you see?"

"Cat-boy?"

"You're a cat alien with manually dilatable pupils and you just said you didn't like it when I came across serious."

"A fair point."

"So?"

He mimicked their 'so?' back to them without the S. "Oh?"

"What do you see?" they prompted, aiming for soft and landing a little north of it. There was no point being harsh, not with both of them trying to stay as un-traumatised as possible, but the fear and the headache and the situation didn't lend to softness.

"Not much. You're about the only luminous thing in here."

"I'm luminous?"

"You didn't know?"

"Is this the reaction of a person who knew?"

"You reflect the world around you."

"Reflecting isn't the same as glowing."

"You're been gleaming with the light of Harrush since you woke up."

Matter looked down at themself but it didn't clarify the point. To their own eyes they formed no light at all. "I don't think other people can see that."

"Huh… You've been brighter… after we met Raxen's vava. The last set of tunnels we were in you barely shone at all."

That would be all the meaningful contact they'd been sharing with Lacha and the others. But maybe that wasn't something to raise in this pit right now with a harrushetti. "Am I at least a decent torch?"

"Not really."

"Ouch."

That pulled a brief laugh out of Brruuh. As his nerves increased, they sparked against Matter's skin like hailstones. With their free hand, they touched at their personal shields, always affixed next to their comms wristband, tucked away and hard to see. And gone. "Ah, fuck!"

"What? Are you hurt?" The panic spiked,

compressing around Matter's chest and stomach and entirely not theirs.

"Nei," they reassured, trying to keep their breathing something resembling even and steady. Wall against their tele-empathy or not, apparently Brruuh needed co-regulation to keep calm here. Did harrushetti hold their kittens? Teach them to breathe? "Sorry, I've just lost my personal…" They trailed off. That was one way to open up the 'you wear personal shields?' conversation and the fact that Matter had been less than completely honest about their tele-empathic score. "Shields," they finished reluctantly.

"I didn't even know you wore personal-shields." He ran the words together, avoiding the s.

Matter let out a little, disarming laugh. "Always."

"You told me you were tele-empathically null."

"I said I was *essentially* null."

"You lied."

"It's complicated."

"You lied."

Ouaeahhn on planet communicated tele-empathically with everything around them, personal shields did little to dim the endless noise of it all. But with non-ouaeahhn it could be more effective. It was often more difficult to build a bond with anyone who wasn't ouaeahhn, like speaking in a language you weren't exactly fluent in. Non-tele-empathic species always thought feelings felt the same person to person, species to species, but if rage could be boiling hot or icy cold depending where you were from the feeling of heat or ice didn't clarify much. And ever since the O.H. mining disaster, Matter had had a harder time building tele-empathic bonds with people, had clung to personal shields like a safe wall to hide within. And between humans being literally null and harrushetti being so naturally shielded they registered as a minus-one on the scale, their tele-empathic status on the ship had been… "I lied."

"Why?"

"Because I was scared, Brruuh. You'd already told me you didn't think I was in a good place to be going for my DeST. I was floundering planet-side, I always do. I can't—" They huffed out a breath. Then took a more even one. These feelings, this current anxiety and trauma, it wasn't theirs. Accept it; let it wash over and through like rain through leaves. Feelings are like weather, they can be strong, they can cause damage, but it each one eases and fades. "Ouaeahhn names are complicated. We start with the second half. My ahni— the feeling of home. More specifically, that feeling when you start recognising the markers of home and you know you're going to be there soon. And then our first half is chosen or given based on what we're like as we grow. I lied about Chamber's interpretation of my name too. Ymma—I am dangerous-potential and movement. If I don't move, I get… dangerous."

"Dangerous how?"

Matter chewed their lip. This was the kind of

conversation they always tried to avoid and a pit on Pitzk with no idea if anyone knew where they were felt even less ideal than any normal place or time to have this conversation. "Have you ever been so tired you keep almost falling asleep? Like the time begins to disappear and you can't remember what happened?"

"Ja."

"You know how you're not supposed to drive in that because it's dangerous?"

"Ja."

"It's exactly that feeling, but it's flight I'm missing rather than sleep."

"That is impossible to understand."

"I told you it was complicated."

Silence settled between them, Brruuh's hand still in Matter's, his emotions still flickering over them. A bond forged with him that was stronger than harrushetti natural shielding. Or maybe it was just Brruuh's history coming into play. For all Matter knew, Brruuh's culture—the YaBin community— were less tele-empathically avoidant than the rest of the planet, but they would never know since everything of them but Brruuh had been destroyed.

"How much do you lie to people?" Brruuh asked, voice quiet almost as if he didn't really want to ask at all. "How easily do you do it? Do you reach for it more quickly than truth?"

Cold washed through Matter, like they'd been

hollowed out entirely.

Brruuh flinched back, breaking the contact between them, removing himself from the feedback loop Matter had been working so hard to manage. Disconnecting from the difficulty of the way he'd made them feel in a way Matter was never offered in return. Resentment boiled inside that concave space Brruuh had dug out with his words. They let it sit. It would pass. Probably.

"We need to get out of here," Matter said, pushing to their feet and holding in the pained noise that wanted to escape. Damage or just pain? Impossible to tell without looking. Still, they couldn't stay here like this. Whether someone was going to eventually come to their rescue or not.

Sauraxen

"**K**eep the predator calm" Sauraxen peeped at Lacha.

"That's *my* job!?"

"Come on, Lacha, please."

Lacha's hair rose around them, fear and panic twisting the strands but they asked, "What do you want me to do?"

"Just pretend to be hurt. He's nice, I promise. He

just needs a task."

"Ow," Lacha lied in ECE, holding out their arm. "I got banged."

Dimae approached, asking if he could take their arm to examine it. Sauraxen peeped her thanks to Lacha, scurrying over to check on anyone else. She invited other wrexi flirting with injury over to request aid from Dimae. With Lacha pinned to his side, hopefully even the most reticent wrexi would let him help.

The tunnels continued to rumble around them, shifting the small cavern they had found themselves in. As far as places to hunker down to wait for those last vestiges of quake to stop, this one wasn't bad. The danger of traversing tunnels while they reshaped and reformed was too great to risk it. Better to regroup here, even if it was a little dank and sulphur-ey. It was cramped too, wrexi practically falling over each other, and poor Dimae having to crouch close to the ground to fit at all as he shifted from one injured wrexi to another.

"You okay?" Ratch asked.

"It's been a while," Sauraxen replied. "Last time something like this happened to me aliens were invading my ship." She rubbed her cheek where there had once been a slice through her scales. All evidence washed away by the magic of modern medicine. If only emotions healed that quickly.

"That doesn't happen here," Ratch reassured. "Who

is going to come to Pitzk?"

Sauraxen tilted her chin up in an attempt at humour, but the amount of times she had wandered into a trafficking trap kept that restless energy alive in her limbs. A problem of sensory vision was that it was all too easy to make a cave-looking thing inviting to a wrexi, especially in a bright space.

Wrexi were rare off Pitzk, Sauraxen had never run across another, and that rarity sparked intrigue. Their appearance was apparently pleasing in two very oddly specific ways and plenty of people had no qualms kidnapping wrexi to keep as pets or for sex, regardless of IPA regulations forbidding such things. The only reason Sauraxen had managed to avoid such a fate was the community she had built around herself. More often than not, Matter was the one storming to her rescue, bloody knuckles and soft hands pulling her out of harm's way. All she wanted now was to run all the way back to Galactic Whale, the safety therein. But she needed the rest of her crew for that to work.

"They'll settle soon," Ratch murmured, seemingly not to Sauraxen at all. "They always do. And then we can get back to celebrating."

Sauraxen snorted. "You weren't celebrating anyway."

"I just like things done properly."

Both wrexi jerked as the rumbles grew closer. Louder where they should have faded. More intense when they should have softened. A new tunnel opened up to a huge, safe and steady seeming area.

On instinct and in a wash, the wrexi surged forward, sweeping Sauraxen and Dimae up with them.

She tried to shout the warning, having been caught in a trap like this enough times. Walking into back rooms and ships and that one time a wicker basket— Matter still hadn't let go of that, teasing Sauraxen like it was a temptation every time they came across a woven storage container. Matter always took it hard. Got so angry and afraid in equal measure. And Sauraxen hadn't understood it before. Not really, too wrapped up in her own shame. But this time, this tunnel that wasn't a tunnel, this cavern that wasn't a cavern, this trap that buzzed with ship engines… She finally felt that fear and anger that Matter had always presented. Because a whole crowd of wrexi had just stormed straight into it. A thing designed to capture them, to prey upon their weakest spots and abuse them.

"What do we do?" Dimae hissed, barely louder than a breath, and cradling a badly hurt wrexi to his chest to keep them safe.

"You keep tending to their wounds, we can figure something out. And keep your head down, if Matter's experience was anything to go by, they'll kill you for not being what they want."

"And you?"

"I'm a wrexi."

"Nei, what are you going to do?"

"It's a ship, isn't it? You do your job, I'll do mine."

"You're an engineer."

"Exactly."

Brruuh

Clawing his way out of a pit on an unfamiliar planet where each step closer to the surface he got filled his lungs with sulphur and made it ever harder to breathe might officially make it to the list of Brruuh's least favourite activities. Doing it with Matter's poorly suppressed, pained panting, their breath hissing through teeth clenched tight, with Matter who had been lying to him about something so serious, so boundary defying the entire time they'd known each other definitely made it that much worse.

It wasn't like Brruuh had expected complete truth from them; the space whale story was beyond obviously a falsification. But when someone told you they were tele-empathically null, essentially or otherwise, it meant no need for shields. What if Matter had been playing with his emotions the entire time? There was no way for Brruuh to actually discover something like that. No way from him to know. How could he ever trust them again after this? And to make it all worse, he had agreed that Sauraxen shouldn't have to give them up, that she could still offer them meaningful contact in a way that directly contradicted Brruuh's entire culture. How was he to confirm that it was his own caring instincts that wanted that to happen? How could he be sure Matter hadn't planted the thought in his head?

He crested the surface of the planet, emerging once again onto the yellow-hazed mountains and hills that covered the outer layer of Pitzk. He turned to offer Matter a hand out of the pit, which they gratefully took. No longer able to suppress the agonised sound that escaped them. Their tele-empathy shot out in a wave, disrupting the sulphur cloud around them and sending a shock of agony through Brruuh that pinned his ears to his head and made him stumble.

West of them, a ship blasted into the void, sending clouds of sulphur billowing in their direction. Brruuh coughed, each inhale brining more aggravating sulphur into his lungs.

"We need to get to the ship," Matter announced. Their voice was rough. Sulphur bothering them just as much as it was Brruuh.

"Who was that?" Brruuh asked, gesturing futilely where mystery ship had been.

Matter grabbed Brruuh's face and turned it toward them, looking into his eyes with an intensity that he had never before seen in anyone, let alone someone as unserious as Matter. "We need to get to the ship, now."

"But we don't even know where the captain—" Over Matter's shoulder a huge creature emerged from the caverns beneath the surface. As wide as the largest tunnel, the creature leapt into the air like a dolphin out of an Earth ocean and dove back down toward Brruuh and Matter. "How are we going to find it in this?" Brruuh asked.

Matter let go of his face and set off in a direction. Brruuh pinned his attention to their back and followed.

In surprisingly short order, with the thunder of a tunnel-creating and horrifying looking worm-thing rumbling behind them, they found the yellow-dusted bobbley beauty that was Galactic Whale. The boarding plank descending for them to rush onto the ship.

"Basti!" Matter cried, throwing their arms around their half-brother as the ship buzzed closed behind them.

"Sau?" Brruuh asked, shaking some of the sulphur off him in a billowing puff like dandelion seeds. Around them the filters of Galactic Whale hummed and huffed, trying to peel the sulphur off them.

"Brruuh," Sau greeted back. "Your captain appears to be kidnapping me."

"Xe is joking," Sebastian clarified. "We need to get

everyone clean before we can do much else. I love my ship but it's not designed for this and we haven't got our engineer back yet."

"We need to get moving," Matter insisted.

"Explain while we try and set the showers to decontam. Wait," he turned to Brruuh, "Can you get wet?"

Brruuh shook his head.

"Could I offer you a hairdryer?"

"I don't know what that is."

"It blows hot air," Matter explained briefly, flicking off the gravity well lest it capture the sulphur off their bodies and throw it straight into the overworking filters, and starting up the ladder to the living floor. Something about their appearance was wrong but Brruuh couldn't begin to have specified what it was.

"Like you," he couldn't help but mutter.

Matter's voice quality changed as the pain of further climbing forced their jaw to clench and their breath to shorten. "For the purpose of drying things faster. It might work without getting you wet but…"

"But it would be easier to contain the water from the shower," Basti explained. "Rather than risking blowing the sulphur off you and into the filters anyway."

"As long as I can get dry, I will likely be well," Brruuh acquiesced.

Showering was a new and decidedly unpleasant experience. Stripping down with the ship's captain, his paramour's parent, and Matter was uncomfortable enough. Basti put all their clothes into a sealable box for the time being as Matter turned on the jets. Brruuh couldn't help the yowl that escaped him when the water first hit. But this water wasn't like the stuff on Harrush that had nearly killed him. This was warm; it passed over him and swirled in yellowed rivulets down the drain.

He lingered in the corner as Matter and Basti conversed, words lost to him in the thunder of water. Everybody else seemed to know what to do, swiping soap or liquids from bottles over themselves to create scented bubbles that washed away the tacky yellow substance. Basti huffed as he poured yet more bubble-liquid into his hands and went back into his hair for a third time.

Matter approached Brruuh, though how one could approach in as cramped a situation as this he didn't know. "Do you want me to do it?" they asked.

Brruuh nodded mutely and stood in silence as Matter's fingers dug into his fur, rubbing in some of that bubble liquid. Only Sauraxen had ever touched him like that and Brruuh was embarrassed and ashamed to find himself leaning into that touch. He shouldn't. He didn't even know where his paramour currently was, though by the way Matter had clamped down on their emotions, he had a sinking suspicion she was on the ship that had flown away.

"We'll get her back," Matter whispered, voice

carrying over the rush of water.

"Is that another lie?" he accused, helpless but to reach for defensive anger.

Matter looked at him again, all that same horrifying seriousness. "Nei. I promised her I wouldn't let anything happen to her and I won't. She is eaalah. Don't you ever ask me that again."

It was with a frown that Matter finished scrubbing the rest of the sulphur from his body. They tossed a terribly fake smile to Sebastian with the words, "Your hairdryer, your problem." Before taking up a surprisingly naked stance in the pilot's console to follow the ship.

Sebastian

Drying Brruuh's fur was… weird. Sebastian had needed to go to his own quarters to retrieve the hair dryer and now the pair of them—and Sau, who was just as naked as ever and rather visibly yellow in the aufenthaltsraum lights—were stood close enough to the botany racks that the plant leaves swayed in the remnant wake of the hot air making Brruuh's fur stand on end.

"The plan," Basti said, because things always felt

less awkward if he was in captain mode. Hopefully Matter would be able to hear most of it from the pilot's console, but they already knew their job. They had been the one to pitch it in the uncomfortable shared shower. "Is we're going to follow the ship with the trafficked wrexi on for as long as we can, while putting out buoy requests for IPA assistance. Ideally we won't have to fight the ship on our own, but if it comes down to it, we're getting those wrexi back one way or another."

Brruuh shivered.

"Sau, could you go to that panel on the wall and press the button with the little plus sign on it?" Basti asked.

Sau scurried over and pressed the button, the little beeps lost to the whoosh of the hairdryer. Maybe turning the ambient temperature in the aufenthaltsraum up wouldn't help Brruuh's core temperature, but Basti would do what he could to keep him from getting sick. After all, they weren't only down an engineer but a medic too.

He tried not to think about the way Matter had looked at him when they said they were certain Sauraxen was on that ship. When they had admitted they couldn't be as sure about Dimae.

A cough wracked his body, bending him at the waist and shoving the hairdryer blast toward Sau instead of Brruuh.

The wrexi shrieked a peep and leapt onto the

dining table.

Brruuh choked on a laugh.

"Well at least I get to tell this story," Sau huffed, climbing back down.

"Sorry," Sebastian offered, throat raw. He returned to the task of getting Brruuh dried off.

Sebastian spent the rest of his day-cycle making sure the ship was as clean as possible, making sure the sulphur had been cleared off any surface it might have lingered on, including using a suction-cleaner on the entirety of the cargo bay and setting the contents of it into another sealed box. What he was going to do with these boxes of Pitzki sulphur he didn't know, but he didn't need to know that now. They could sit there for years if necessary.

As the lights changed to the night cycle and another cough burst out of Basti's lungs, he made his way back to the aufenthaltsraum for food.

"You have to sleep eventually," Matter said. Their voice was soft, no accusation in the words.

"How am I supposed to do that?" Basti huffed, looking up and surprised to find them in a pair of his lounging trousers and no shirt, hair still loose around their shoulders. Something was... off, but he couldn't begin to name what.

"You think I don't understand?" Matter asked, that same softness lingering in their words.

"It's not your Bond Mate that's missing. I don't even know if he's still on the planet."

"If he's still on the planet, he's safe until we can go back for him. He'll get a message out to us from the broadcasting tower and it'll be fine."

"I know going after them is the right choice," Sebastian snapped. No matter how bad it made him feel. No matter how stressed and worried and lonely he was.

"Top ten ways to make me feel bad that I need to ask you for something," Matter joked.

Basti sighed. "I'm sorry. What's up?"

"You don't happen to have a spare personal shield lying around, do you?"

He shook his head. Being tele-empathically null, and with a crew made up of a majority of the same, he hadn't even considered getting spares.

Matter breathed out slowly. "Alright. Thanks anyway."

"What do you need a shield for?"

Matter paused, opened their mouth and closed it. Their eyebrows drew together. They shook their head and smiled at Basti. "It's just easier to have it as a backup. I'll be fine. We'll all be fine. But only if you sleep."

"I can't… I can't go into that room."

"Sleep in mine."

"And where will you sleep?"

"Luckily enough, those beds are big enough for two. Or I'll crash out after you're up again if you want the privacy. Or there's a fair few spare quarters we've never used."

"How can you be so calm about this?"

"I'm not."

"You seem it."

Matter took hold of Basti's hand, concentration plain on their face. A wash of foreign stress overwhelmed him, filling him and overflowing like hot water in a cup. And hot on its heels agony blasted like fireworks across his joints. And then it was gone as Matter disengaged.

"You're right," Basti agreed, resolve strengthening. "We'll get them back. There is nei other option."

Tracking
Day 1

Sauraxen

Being in a cargo bay with a thousand-ish panicked wrexi and nowhere to go, on a ship headed for who-knew where, all the while trying to hide a harrushetti who was practically three times the height of even the tallest wrexi amongst them was the kind of pressure Sauraxen hadn't faced since her MSc engineering exam when the invigilators had refused to turn the lights down. Oh, and the lights were really bright here too. None of which was helped by the wrexi panic pressing against her own need to flee—to run and run and run until she found a safe space. Sauraxen tried to smush down that desire, leaned into the knowledge that she had options beyond running. No matter how much it felt like she was lifting all of her scales to sit on end—a physical impossibility. No matter what intrinsic instincts she was battling to do it. She'd gone to Matter for help with this feeling once, this desire and instinct to flee, automatic panic response. Matter had suggested seeking something comforting. But that only came after Sauraxen had sought out potential solutions here.

Her wristband wasn't working. The comms portion offering only the depressing bloop-bloop that denoted no signal. Which meant the ship had a signal jammer somewhere. Which means she and Dimae were going to have to figure out another solution on their own with no guarantee anyone on the outside would be able to find them.

How exactly Sauraxen and Dimae were meant to figure this out in amongst a horde of panicking wrexi she didn't know. Dimae was stuck tucked away in a corner, actively treating injured wrexi while letting out quiet calming purrs to try and keep people around him comfortable. It worked, because more wrexi had started huddling closer to the known predator.

Sauraxen slipped through the crowd and paused by him. "Nei signal anywhere," she whispered in ECE. "I can't find access to a signal jammer either. This place is stuck together really well and I didn't exactly take a bunch of tools down to the planet." Even if she had, she wouldn't have been wearing them at her naming ceremony,

Dimae dipped a hand into one of his belt pouches, the medical one, and pulled out a shiningly sharp scalpel with a cap to cover the tip.

Sauraxen let out a disbelieving pip.

"It's an effective tool," Dimae said. "And good for self-defence."

"I have nei ability to fight."

He shrugged a shoulder. "Then just use it as a tool."

She took the blade and examined the tip. That could function as a screwdriver, right? She made her way back over to the only section of screws she had found thus far in her investigations. There was no guarantee it would lead anywhere at all, let alone anywhere useful, but it could lead Sauraxen into the mechanics of the ship. And if she could get into that, there was a chance she could do some real damage.

She had to take what chance she could. Because, even if Matter was coming, Sauraxen couldn't wait to be rescued by them this time. She had to get herself out of trouble.

Tracking

Day 2

Brruuh

Brruuh's datapad blinked a light slowly at Brruuh. A message to him sitting in his office for who knew how long. For all Brruuh knew it could have come in immediately after landing on Pitzk. Not that it was going to be something important, something relevant, something he wanted to deal with right now. With his paramour being trafficked away from him, and them illegally following that trafficking ship, and the lingering icy cold that seemed to have settled below his fur from the shower. With the tension still crackling between him and Matter…

He opened the message.

```
Brruuh,
I was surprised to hear from you after
all this time. Thank you for the apology,
though it isn't necessary. I was upset at
the time but I think I managed the
eyebrowless look quite handsomely.
I'm stationed on Njao-Ehxedij—we've
taken to calling it Cheddar like the
cheese in ECE because the xedij part kind
of sounds like it and humans are like
that. I remember you used to despair at
that habit when everyone started calling
you Dr Tea instead of Brruuh. What have
you been pulled into the orbit of lately?
Vedran.
```

Brruuh stared at the message for a long time. He'd almost forgotten sending the message to Vedran in the first place. Opening a social conversation as a stepping stone to potentially requesting help with the provisional stamp glittering across all their Deep Space Travel Licenses. Now…

```
Vedran,
I'm glad to hear back from you and that
the situation with the birthday cake has
transformed into a humorous anecdote
rather than a memory with sharp edges.
I've actually joined a small crew on a
cargo runner.
```

Maybe he shouldn't go into all the details about how he had been assigned as their DST license assessor and grew too close to leave the ship. How they had brought him back from the brink of death the way only a family was supposed to be able to for a harrushetti. Matter always did say Ahthae was just like family…

It's a chaotic sort of place. A lot of culture clashes for a small crew.

The fact that he was still unable to get past the ease with which Matter lied. The fact that they had been holding something so important as tele-empathic links back from him. Made worse by the way he had felt that agony radiating out from them on the surface of Pitzk.

If Dimae was here he could have asked about it, asked about tele-empathic links with ouaeahhn. But with Dimae missing, presumed on the ship they were following, Brruuh was on his own. He didn't even have any family to write home to for help.

He hesitated, stylus hovering over the send button. Should he wait until they had finished chasing down the traffickers? Would it be too risky to send out what seemed like casual conversation? Was it too callous?

He tapped the screen, letting the message begin its journey toward Njao-Ehxedij.

Tracking
Day 3

Matter

Matter's whole body shook. Pain throbbed down one leg and across their torso but they couldn't locate any specific source. They tried to ignore the way their memories kept surging up, playing out in front of them in those unfocused moments as they followed in the wake of the ship that had stolen at least Sauraxen and probably Dimae too.

Would they be in the kind of danger Matter had

faced? Would they be desperately deprived of everything they needed to survive? Locked in isolation?

They shook off the idea. This wouldn't be like that. They weren't stealing survival hormones from the wrexi, they were going to sell them to people outside the IPA who wanted them for their cuteness or their aesthetic appeal. People with no care that these 'pets' were people with advanced intelligence.

The comms bleep yanked Matter out of their thoughts once again. Sebastian had set up a bouncing IPA private communication to drop at regular intervals. Each one included the experience of being in the tunnels, his interaction with the people who wanted to traffic those wrexi, people who had chosen to leave him and Sau because of Sau's illness and Basti's humanity. Each message included Matter's knowledge of the ship, its registration number and every other detail they had been able to claw out of their terrified mind.

Matter had barely left the pilot's console. Had dipped into the aufenthaltsraum to grab food they could eat at the controls, they'd even fallen asleep in the chair once or twice. Unable to take their eyes off the trail of that ship for any decent length of time. But with every pinsect of space traversed, they almost wished Sebastian had left the IPA out of it. It would have been okay if the IPA had got back to them, or if Matter could guarantee the trafficking ship didn't pick up their message, or if Matter had any level of control. The uncertainty, knowing the risk that the IPA could care more about their unlicensed travel than about the trafficking ship, not knowing if they were going to have to figure this out alone, it came in waves of vibrating intensity stealing Matter's breath. And with each quiet bleep announcing another comm drop, Matter's paranoia increased. Their ability to do more than chase down the ship decreased.

The pilot's console seemed to shrink around them, the bubble of clear space-worthy glass all too substantial in the face of what had happened to Matter all those years ago.

This time it was a too-loud voice over comms yanking them back. "It says here you're travelling without a license."

"Fuck," Matter yelped. They'd forgotten Sauraxen still hadn't got around to fixing the volume of communications in the pilot's console. Would she ever be able to now?

"Ja, it's unfortunate. Can you offer an explanation or...?"

"It's an emergency," Matter ground out, frustrated to find the ship communicating with them was the kind that opened comms without receiving ships permission. They glanced over at the reading about it. 2-Eas a pah-rushi vessel designed to chart the unchartered. Enough security to take a little bug-like Galactic Whale in but not nearly enough to take down a trafficking ring. "We're tracking a trafficking operation. Did you not find our report?"

"What kind of emergency leads to a cargo trawler without its full DeST obviously leaving Pitzk when they're supposed to be grounded at Gnarresh-Fle, ninety-three tonish from here, chasing down a trafficking operation?"

Good to know their ship readout details were much more thorough than Matter's. "Medical."

"We can tow you to the nearest IPA medi-centre."

"And how would that help prevent the trafficking exactly?"

"Tracking trafficking really isn't your job."

"I really don't give a shit if it's my job. You think I'm just going to toss this into wider IPA hands? When it takes six to eight standard weeks to expect a response at all? They'd be long gone by then, probably out of IPA space at all."

"Look, I know trafficking is a real issue, but you travelling illegally isn't actually helping."

"You can either help us or leave me alone."

"Unfortunately that's not how the IPA works." There was amusement in the tone.

Matter huffed. If Basti wasn't about to actually make them second officer, he could handle pissy IPA agents. They leaned back in their chair and called, "Basti?"

"Basti?" the IPA agent repeated. "Basti Jones?"

"Who is this?"

"It's Benoit."

"Benoit? Hi, it's Matter."

"Matter!" Benoit cheered. "Long time nei see. You wanna restock while you tell me about the trafficking?"

"What happened to taking us to the nearest IPA Station? What happened to us not helping?"

"I reckon I can get it past the security chief."

"Why's that?"

"You could probably bribe him with some Jones Farm coffee beans that I know Basti keeps on board."

"Good luck with that, he won't even let me drink it."

Benoit

The bobbly ship was coated in bright yellow sulphur, dislodging some as it settled into the landing bay of the 2-Eas. The belly opened up to release the crew from its confines. A grey striped harrushetti, a wrexi with some signs of age from what little Benoit knew about them, Matter in an olive green jumpsuit and, "Bas!" Benoit surged forward to wrap his upper limbs around Basti in an enormous hug.

"Benoit!" the human cried back, clinging a little tighter than Benoit was used to these days.

"Careful," Benoit teased. "Too much of that and Dimae will get jealous."

For a second, Basti crumpled. Then he pulled away, all serious, firm set to his jaw. "I need to talk to you about that."

"Did something happen?"

Basti covered his mouth to cough, the air around him tinting yellow with each expulsion.

"Let's get you all to medi-bay," Benoit declared, not waiting for a response before he started herding the small crew into the corridor.

"I'm fine," Basti protested. "But I do have a crew member who needs medical attention."

"Crew member, am I?" the wrexi asked, Earth Common Eurean accented but clear.

"I need to take names," Benoit said. "Then we can get you all checked out and helped and start figuring out what comes next."

"Nuh-uh," Matter snapped. Looking at them made Benoit's feathers itch. Memories of finding them in that cage flashing in front of his eyes. He pushed them away. "We need to get after that ship. Nei waiting."

"Give me the codes and I'll send them up to the pilots."

Matter rattled off a ship code for Benoit to blast across via ship comms.

"Names," Benoit demanded.

"Sebastian LeaYaPar-Jones, human, EC.623, captain. Ymmattrahni of Ouaeahhn, ouaeahhn, pilot. Brruuh TeaYaBin, harrushetti, cognitivist. And Sau of Pitzk, wrexi and… guest."

"Where's Dimae?" Benoit asked as he filled out the requisite security forms, paying half attention to the route to medi-bay.

"On the trafficking ship you need to be following," Brruuh answered, similarly accented ECE. His voice was rough. Damage or nature?

"I've sent the details to our piloting team. Why don't you tell me what's going on until you're cleared to do as you feel necessary."

Benoit could not possibly have been prepared for the story told in three between Basti, Matter, and Brruuh. The idea that traffickers could be so bold as to land on an IPA planet and actively dig to find such a huge amount of people. It was one thing to pick people up here and there, schemes of opportunity like the one that had taken Matter, but something this large? And this blatant inside IPA borders?

"Any allergies to speak of?" one of the 2-Eas medical officers asked as soon as the group entered, already accessing their IPA medical records that Benoit had sent forth.

"Nei," Basti responded. "Oh, wait. Bugs."

"That's new," Benoit muttered, glad to have something else to do with his brain while it attempted to process the information. He'd already sent the full set of notes to Captain Hazai as a follow-up to the request to chase that mystery ship.

"Ja, it's really mild," Basti said. "But apparently the feelings I was feeling aren't just normal ones."

Benoit's wings fluttered in amusement.

"Don't you start," Basti grumbled.

"I didn't say anything."

"You don't have to say anything, I can see you." He coughed again, body wracked and shaking with it. Benoit helped him onto one of the medi-centre bends, letting him sit atop the IPA standard green blanket.

"Why are you coughing up sulphur?" Benoit tried not to eye the grey striped harrushetti, who was, in the brighter light of medi-bay, also tinged yellow.

"The atmosphere of Pitzk," Sau explained. "We weren't meant to be exposed to the surface without precautions but…" xe trailed off. But someone hadn't cared about leaving survivors.

"I'll go speak with the captain," Benoit promised. "Get this sorted out." It wasn't what the 2-Eas was for, but sometimes emergencies necessitated change. Hopefully Hazai would see it the same way he did. "I'll be back."

Captain Hazai was in her office, wings neatly folded behind her back. She greeted Benoit in Pah-Ruhki with, "I got your report. We're not meant for this. How much of your desire for exception is based in your history?"

Benoit's wings twitched to wrap around him in a

protective hug. "Some," he admitted. "Trafficking is a personal sore spot for me." And the reason he had left IPA strike teams. "But we both know there isn't another ship in this area of space. Could we trust that someone else would be able to step in in time?"

"Do you know this ship? Galactic Whale—what a title!"

"I do. The captain and the pilot are old friends." He, like so many people he knew, had met Matter through Basti. Specifically, going with Basti for a local EC.623 holiday that Matter had also been attending. They'd hit it off right away, but Basti would always be the closer friend. Even if Matter's presence didn't make his feathers itch.

"Then you know somebody else is going to have to do their security checks."

"Right. Does that need to happen before we start following the ship?"

Hazai's feathers flared. "You just focus on getting someone else to do their security check for now."

He wanted to argue. Wanted to demand or beg or convince Hazai to send the pilots after the ship immediately, no security screenings necessary. But that wasn't how this ship worked. Better to get the needed checks done quickly so they could shift. "Yes captain."

Brruuh

"I'm getting strange readings off you," one of the doctors said to Brruuh. He and the others from Galactic Whale had been set up in their own beds, though Matter had immediately abandoned theirs to sit with Sau. The pair leaning close to one another, shoulders pressed together.

"Ah," Brruuh mused. The lingering effects of his near death experience no doubt. Just like the previous near-death experience had left him with some kitten-traits he could never grow out of. But how to raise that? And how to do it without throwing the crew of Galactic Whale into more trouble than they were already in? Without the risk of the 2-Eas medical officers demanding to detour to an IPA medi-centre? Because none of them could risk such a detour.

Matter's head tipped back in a wrexi smile at something Sau had said and an idea struck Brruuh.

"I had an unfortunate run in with a trans-orbital octopus."

"What?"

Matter glanced over at him, suspicion mixing with joy.

"A trans-orbital octopus," Brruuh repeated. "What they do is, they wrap their tentacles around you and press tighter and tighter." He lifted his hands, laying one atop the other and squeezing his fingers tight. "Ja," he sighed. "I'm just recovering from that."

Matter tried to suppress a laugh as the medical officer muttered something in Pah-Ruhki. She stopped in front of Matter, forcing them away from Sau who squinted in the bright light.

"If you think I'm going to make you a trans-orbital octopus for your next gift giving situation," Matter started, ignoring the medical situation in front of them. "I feel it's only fair to warn you I'm really bad at crafts."

The doctor's scanner beeped some warning noises.

"Anyway," they hopped to their feet. "I should get to the pilots here and let them know where we're going."

"Wait," the doctor exclaimed, grasping Matter around the forearm. Matter's grimace spoke of pain the rest of them was hiding. "You can't go anywhere."

Matter gestured at Basti and Sau. "Those two need your attention. I doubt your instruments are calibrated for someone like me and most of those warnings are about my incurable chronic condition." They pulled a box of pain killers from the pocket of their jumpsuit and shook it. It sounded notably emptier than the last time Brruuh had heard it. "I've got management right here."

"You're on the verge of dying!"

Matter smiled sardonically. "It's really not that bad."

Brruuh surged to his own feet, following after them as they left eh medi-bay. "Matter." He laid a hand on their shoulder, not a restriction, a request. "Is it really as bad as that?"

They rubbed their face, pausing but not turning around. "I'm just stressed. It's always worse when I'm stressed. This is…"

"Triggering?" he supplied.

"Dr Brruuh," they teased weakly.

"Regardless of what's going on between us," Brruuh said slowly. Regardless of his interpersonal animosity, his hurt feelings. "You can't ask for contact from Axen, Basti is unwell, this whole episode is akin to your experiences. I understand the necessity. I am—"

"Don't," Matter snapped.

"Don't what?"

"Don't start offering me things you don't want to offer. If you're only doing it because you think I'll die if you don't, that contact ceases to be meaningful. You're pissed at me for lying, I can feel it in the contact—curse of a true Ahthae bond. I get it. At least do me the credit of not trying to pretend so you don't feel guilty if I get hurt or…"

"Or?"

"I just want to get Sauraxen back, everything else

can be fixed."

"Can it? Or are you going to push yourself too far beyond your limits? To the point of further permanent injury? And don't think you can lie to me about this again."

"I do not understand why you're taking this so hard, Brruuh. Of course I lied to you! I didn't know you then."

"But you never corrected it! You never came to me and explained that eventually or in particular circumstances it might change."

"I did tell you that."

"And then you deflected, like you always do. You moved the conversation away from the difficult thing to keep whatever wall between us and you never bothered to—"

"When would I have?" they interrupted.

"Oh, I don't know, any of the many months we spent together on Galactic Whale?" Work time, casual time, he couldn't begin to count the amount of time the pair of them had spent lounging on the sofas in the aufenthaltsraum just talking about nothing serious. "The time while we were on Gnarresh-Fle after I had joined the crew?" When he and Matter had run across one another late into the night-cycle and ended up settling together with a puzzling vid-game. "You had plenty of chances."

"The IPA doesn't go for exceptions. It doesn't have a box for 'well in certain circumstances this is different'. Rules are rules and the box is either ticked or it's not."

"I am not the IPA in person-form."

"Ugh, how did we even end up in this argument right now? I have a task, a job only I can do. Go back to medi-bay, Brruuh, and leave me alone."

Tracking
Day 4

A hand on their arm yanked Matter unceremoniously from the doze they'd collapsed into. "It's shift change," the axelaxe owner of the hand in question murmured in ECE.

The piloting console on the 2-Eas was a traditional shape for a pah-rushi vessel: set away from the rest of the command centre and with at least three pilots on duty at any given time, each with their own designated task. Each pilot had their own bubble, large enough to spread even the widest of wingspans. They had welcomed Matter easily enough; nobody sensible would refuse a ouaeahhn pilot with the ability to follow the trails ships left in their passage through space. One of the side pilots had acquiesced their console, folding out the back rest they slid down to accommodate wings that Matter didn't have.

The other two had chatted with each other amicably enough in Pah-Ruhki, the trills and whirrs a background noise as Matter watched the ship's trail and marked it on the star chart in front of them. denoting other interesting regional details, this was a charting ship after all.

Pah-rushi people retained a lot of their birdlike features beyond the wings. Instead of hair, they had a blast of feathers. Their eyes were that circular shape Matter was more used to seeing on birds from EC.623, with less frequent blinks that humans or harrushetti. Though, at least Matter was used to no blinking from wrexi so it wasn't as disconcerting as others had explained it to be at first. The real thing that denoted a pah-rushi was, of course, the wings. A huge pair sprouting from each of their backs, large enough and strong enough to carry at least themself if not a passenger too.

Why was an axelaxe on a pah-rushi vessel? Would xe have to mist xemself down each morning before starting a shift? Or were the statements of axelaxe amphibious needs exaggerated? Xyr hand wasn't wet.

"I can't," Matter protested.

The pink and purple frills around xyr head swayed

softly as xe tugged lightly on Matter's arm. "I have three ways to get you out of that chair. One: simply inform you that it's against ship regulations to allow an unrested pilot to remain on duty. Two: remind you that you'll be nei use if you work yourself into the undertow, you already fell asleep once. Or three: I can pick you up and carry you out of here if need be." That last threat came with the peek of teeth: a threat of a smile.

"My friend is out there."

The axelaxe crouched, eyes taking on a distant quality. Emotions flared against Matter's skin, sinking into them just enough to show the axelaxe had lowered xyr shields. "I understand. But you're going to be far better help if you're rested enough to be called upon when it's really important. Our pilots are highly trained. We chart the uncharted, remember?"

"If I'm not here, how can I be sure they'll keep going?"

"Jenji, you're following that trafficking ship, right?"

"Those are the orders," Jenji answered from the primary piloting console in the centre of the room.

"You'll keep on this mission until we get them?"

Jenji glanced over. "Overriding captains orders?"

The axelaxe's frills flicked.

"I'll let you know before any potential changes take effect, Ezeks."

"Thanks Jenji."

Matter let Ezeks lead them out into the hallway.

Followed xyr soft-scaled footsteps back toward the docking bay. But they stalled as soon as they reached the ahni of it, the area they started to recognise on the ship. "I don't know if I can…"

"Don't know if you can what?"

"If I can go back to my ship. I…" That argument with Brruuh weighed on them. The weight of the emotions of the Ahthae while they still had no personal shields to speak of.

"You're all stressed."

"And she's supposed to be there. Nian. How do I do this without her?" Betraying human tears spilled down Matter's cheeks.

"Whoa, hey." Ezeks scooped Matter into xyr arms.

"What if I lose her?"

Xe squeaked something in axelaxis, an idiom Matter wasn't familiar with, but the wash of comfort via tele-empathic bond soothing in a way only fellow tele-empaths could ever hope to be. "Let's go to my room instead."

Reversing direction, Matter found themself quickly settled in a simple but spacious cabin. The humidity of it washed against their skin in a way that felt like EC.623, the Jones farmstead. The bed's headboard pressed up against a wall, at an angle to the door with a little dressing screen to hide at least part of it from initial view.

"I'm Ezeks, by the way, if you didn't catch it." Xe dipped to open a low cupboard door.

"Matter."

"Good name. What does it mean in its intended language?"

"Movement and."

"And what?" Ezeks asked, risking again with a basket of pre-packaged snacks.

Matter found themself smiling. "It's a nickname. It literally means 'movement and' the rest gets cut off."

"Okay." Ezeks sat on the bed, gesturing for Matter to join xem. "What does it expand into."

"The feeling of home. Specifically when you start to recognise the signs of home, that feeling you get when you know the route from here by heart." Should they mention the danger part that preceded the Matter part? "It's also the ECE word for the stuff that makes up the universe, but I always forget that one." They only remembered because Lacha had said it. Was Lacha also on the trafficking ship? Or still on Pitzk with nei idea what had happened to everyone else?

"Wow, Ezeks just means deep water. But we put a lot of stock in name meanings on Laxe."

"Deep water is a great name meaning," Matter countered. "It would be Laniou in ouaeahhn."

Ezeks leaned over to close the gap between them, pressing xyr shoulder gently against Matter. "I've got access to every vid on the ship servers, you wanna fall asleep watching something and eating too many snacks?"

Benoit

"What are you doing?" The question came from the wrexi Basti had brought with him, the one who had joked about not being crew. Sau.

"We're washing the sulphur off your ship," Benoit explained. Though, in this particular instance, the 'we' was him alone. Hazai had ordered him off security, but he still had a working shift to get through.

"Why?"

"Pitzki sulphur is adhesive. It sticks to things. The risk of carrying it into other IPA ports can be dangerous for some species. Like kil or vetasque. We can't risk it as an IPA charting vessel and Galactic Whale would need to be cleaned up before it could land anywhere else too."

"It's that dangerous?"

"Definitely."

"But we live there."

"You are probably evolutionarily immune or resistant to it. Not the case for everyone."

Sau let out a low trill. "Can I assist?"

"Sure." Benoit passed over a second washing wand. "You point the non-hose end at the ship and press the lever,"

Sau started immediately, blasting a clear path through the yellow coating the ship.

"The sulphur is a huge reason you need a license to travel to Pitzk at all. You're supposed to have really advanced shielding to employ as you enter the atmosphere and deactivate as you leave."

"Like you leave the sulphur where it is on the planet?" Sau clarified.

Or shaking water off your feathers before you entered the nest. "Exactly."

Sau paused to breathe slowly, catching xemself on xyr thighs.

"Are you okay?"

"Oh, I'm just dying."

"What? What? Wait, what?" Benoit found himself in a chirping loop, barely able to keep his words in ECE.

"It's a terminal illness. I don't know the word in ECE. It's what Sauraxen came home for."

"Because you're dying?"

Sau sighed and picked up the wand again, peeling off not just sulphur but the space gunk beneath with a methodical focus Benoit could only dream of. "I wish I hadn't called her now."

"Nei," Benoit insisted.

"It's my fault she's in this situation. That they illegally left that station and, even if we get her back, which I don't even know that I'll live to see, she's still going to be stuck in trouble for coming to visit at all."

"But… But she would…"

"She was never going to come back to Pitzk," Sau continued. "She wouldn't have known really."

"Don't you send messages?" Benoit was always sending messages back to his siblings on Pah-Rush.

"When I can get them to the broadcast station, which is rare and difficult. She would have assumed something was wrong with it and then it would have slipped her mind and we could all have avoided this whole drama."

"But the traffickers would still have come to Pitzk," Benoit argued. "And nobody would have known. Let alone a ship as uniquely qualified to chase them down as this one." Even if Benoit had no idea how they were going to take the ship out with what the 2-Eas had to its name.

Sau peeped and chirped, obviously speaking a language Benoit didn't know. "If the sulphur doesn't kill you, what will?"

"Huh?"

"It's a wrexi idiom. As far as I can tell most cultures have a version of it."

"If the sulphur doesn't kill you what will?" Benoit mused. "If you survive the fall, you can fly again."

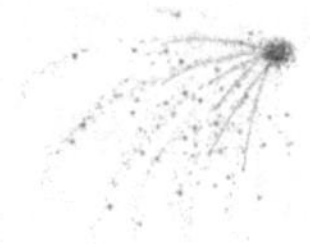

Dimae

It was hard to tell how much time passed on the ship with no day-night cycling to the lights. The endless brightness of it bothered Dimae; he could only imagine how much worse it was for the wrexi trapped with him. Still, sometimes sleep came and other times it didn't. More often than not he was kept awake by the increasing stench of stress and tension emanating from the wrexi around him. No food came to them, Dimae's stomach clenching with hunger he couldn't hope to satiate, not that food appropriate for wrexi— primarily omnivorous with the occasional addition of bugs—would be suitable for him as an obligate carnivore.

Dimae's secondary vocal cords were raw from trying to maintain a calming purr and his eyes burned from being awake too long, when Sauraxen reappeared at his side.

He flinched at the suddenness of her appearance.

"I need you to crawl into the tunnel I made," she whispered. "My claws aren't strong enough to break through a cable."

"What about the scalpel?"

"It's gone."

It was only then that the sharp scent of blood stung Dimae's nose. He flicked his attention over Sauraxen, searching for injuries and finding green blood splattered up her forearms and bare chest.

"What happens if we break the cable?"

"I'm not sure, I think it'll stall the ship."

"You think they're following us?"

"If anyone can find us it's Matter."

And Sebastian would never leave him. Dimae pushed to four feet and let Sauraxen guide him to the tunnel. He wanted to ask about the blood. Wanted to know what had happened. If she was okay. If she needed what little medical care he could offer. But urgency tugged at him. His duty of care extended to the whole group of wrexi, and sabotaging the ship would do more for them than taking the time to treat Sauraxen's cuts. He didn't have much left in his medical supplies pouch anyway, having used almost all of it on the injuries the other wrexi had sustained.

The tunnel was cramped, dug out only large enough for Sauraxen to slither through. He dug his claws into the metal in front of him and dragged himself through the narrow space. Cables and ship innards surrounded him, making him feel like nothing so much as a microbe crawling through a person's insides. Perhaps his job and Sauraxen's weren't as different as he had always imagined.

A large cable blocked his path, preventing further travel. Expanding his pupils to the fullest extent, he could make out what little damage Sauraxen had managed. Some superficial scratches and what appeared to be a bite mark on the outside.

With the precision that came from medical

training, Dimae slid one claw across the cable's casing, revealing the interior cables. They didn't buzz with the threat of dangerous electricity, but Dimae still wrapped his hands around the covered pieces of cable to start pulling them apart anyway.

Outside the tunnel, a ruckus began, the sound of it echoing down the tunnel to press against the soft hairs inside Dimae's ears. Something grabbed at Dimae's feet. He gripped the cable tighter as an unbearable strength yanked him from the space.

Tracking
Day 6

The 2-Eas medical team had been reluctant to let Basti or Sau out of their sights, especially after Matter's sudden abscondment. But with Brruuh's return and leveraging his experience within IPA medical fields, he managed to convince them to let the pair back onto Galactic Whale with some spare portable air filters to keep sucking up the excess sulphur. And the promise that they would check in with medi-bay every day.

Which left Basti and Sau mostly lounging on the sofas in the aufenthaltsraum feeling sorry for themselves while an air filter hummed in the background of any conversation. Though Sau was holding up far better than Basti for some reason. To the extent that the wrexi disappeared for a wander around at least once a day too. Basti, on the other hand, could barely make conversation without devolving into hacking coughs that hurt his ribs and stomach and everything else. He didn't dare look at himself in the ships mirrors lest he discover he looked as bad as he felt. What was this? A sulphur allergy? Or was Pitzk just that inhospitable? He hadn't thought they were on the surface that long. And Brruuh seemed to be fine. And he hadn't even seen Matter for days.

Worst of it all, though were the dreams. The endless repeating moment in that dank cavern with Sau, struggling for breath, when those two bright lights appeared in the darkness as the world rumbled around them. Like two huge eyes blinking at him. He had thought, at first, that it was a hallucination, that he was so badly concussed that he was seeing things. But still, hoping for rescue, Basti had tried calling out, his voice barely making any noise over the din of the quake. And then, that one sentence from the direction of those lights, 'That one's broken, leave it'. And the lights disappearing back into the darkness, leaving him and Sau behind as the world once again crumbled around them.

And every time he awoke from those nightmares

in a soft bed on his ship, he reached instinctively for Dimae only to find him absent.

Not that Basti was making it down to the captain's quarters, or even into Matter's offered room. No, most of the time he slept on the sofas. It wasn't like anyone here would mind; Brruuh and Matter barely ever came back anyway.

Benoit, at least, swung by most days, talking about generic ship happenings, making sure Basti had food and that he'd checked in with medi-bay.

And just like with any other sickness, all Basti wanted was for Dimae to comfort him and pet his hair and purr and tell him it would be over soon.

Matter

Ezeks had followed them onto their allowed piloting shift, had settled xemself against a wall in the room and started tossing around banter with the other two pilots on duty, apparently appointing xemself Matter's personal guard or something. What was xyr job on the ship?

Matter mostly ignored the conversation, focused on the void through the surprisingly small window, focused on trying to remember the relative size of this ship compared to Galactic Whale, focused on remembering their piloting training for this system. In Galactic Whale, the ship moved as soon as Matter wanted it to, the 2-Eas by comparison, had to be prepared three tethroi in advance. Each movement laid into a system that sat on a little green screen in front of each pilot console.

Matter's ouaeahhn vision bounced across comets noses and tails, lingered in the glitter from a star close to turning to its demise. Their fingers flew to record it, more out of habit than anything else. The primary charter in the piloting unit tweeted appreciatively—at least Matter thought it was appreciation, Benoit was the only pah-rushi they'd spent any time with and he didn't make a lot of happy noises around them these days.

Had they wrecked what they had built with Brruuh like that too? Broken a bond before it could fully form? And when they got Sauraxen back, then what? If they got Sauraxen back...

Would Brruuh be willing to move on if they could use Sauraxen as a buffer? Would he want to pull that wall between Sauraxen and Matter like so many of her previous partners had? Would Matter survive it?

The bond Ezeks had carefully forged between them flared with support and care. Matter glanced at xem. Xe flicked xyr frills. Xe had convinced Matter to meet with one of the medical officers outside medi-bay when xe had seen the human-like bruising mottling their skin. With a lot of persuasion and a little bribery, Matter had agreed to let one come to Ezeks' room. Resetting their shoulder, knee, and ankle had thrown stars into their vision and made both the doctor and Ezeks respond as the emotion flared around them. The medical officer had carefully stuck tape to Matter's skin that pressed each of those joints into their proper place and held them there. And that had been that, they'd been back on Ezeks' bed with the axelaxe snuggling close and persuading them to take some pain relief and sleep so their joints could heal, telling them that xe would take a work shift off to stay in contact. When they woke up it was better. It didn't *feel* better. But it was.

They turned their attention back to the small piloting window and frowned. "Something's changed."

"What do you mean?" Ezeks asked, on xyr feet with speed Matter envied. Xe peered out of the window, as if it would illuminate anything to xem.

"The ship stopped," Matter explained. The tail of it ended abruptly, too abruptly for anything but an emergency stop.

"They reached their destination?" one of the pilots asked.

"Nei," Matter said slowly. "They're not at a planet or moon or anything. And there's nei sign of another ship coming."

"They could be shielded," the pilot said.

"Not from me," Matter countered. Even a ghost-shielded ship made trails and wakes in space. "Nei. They... I think they broke down?"

"Aren't trafficking ships usually in meticulous condition?" Ezeks asked.

"Ja," Matter confirmed. It was part of avoiding getting called in. If the ship was in perfect condition with no visible or scannable faults, they wouldn't get picked up by any patrols, were more likely to cross borders without investigation. Even this ship had shed its sulphur trail after a day or so.

The only way it could have broken down was if somebody sabotaged it.

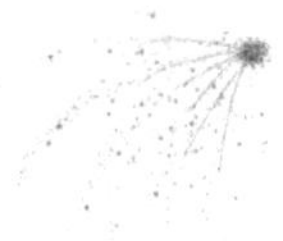

Brruuh

Brruuh had always found work to be the most comforting thing. It definitely wasn't the most mentally healthy choice, but Brruuh knew the base of the decision and now didn't seem the best time to try and wrangle his mental health around work as well as his mental health around his paramour's kidnapping. So, instead of working on himself, Brruuh had offered his services to the ship's cognitivist. Mostly, he ended up on reports and certification duty, but sitting in an office with another IPA cognitivist while filling out and filing away reports was like stepping back into his life on a Station before he got assigned to run the assessment on the ship that was now Galactic Whale. A life he had fully intended to return to before forging bonds he never expected to find.

He exchanged further messages with Vedran, not yet mentioning the problem that made him reach out in the first place, instead trying to enjoy the interaction. Vedran talked through his latest problem with the extremists beginning to make themselves known on his station, and Brruuh talked through some of his issue with Matter's dishonesty. Brruuh revelled in conversation with someone else who understood cognitivism as extensively as he did. Even if Vedran had offered up the annoying and perfectly logical suggestions of 'talk to them about it' and 'why do you think this has upset you so much?' followed up with the dreaded, 'do you really think they're that untrustworthy? Or are you being mean because you feel hurt?'—not that Brruuh could do anything with these suggestions since Matter had been absent since their argument in the corridor outside the 2-Eas medi-bay.

Spending the last three days on the 2-Eas should have been uncomfortable, not just because of the situation at hand, but because Brruuh was a cat on a ship full of birds. But nobody seemed to mind his presence in the common areas; they even invited him into activities and their VR contest. In previous positions, Brruuh had gently rebuffed such offers wherever possible. He liked his privacy, his own space. But here, he took people up on the invitations. Surrounding himself with busy crew, going about their lives like nothing was wrong, gave Brruuh spaces to process in a way he couldn't have spending time on Galactic Whale where Sauraxen's absence rubbed his fur raw.

He was in one of the silly contests, flipping round game-counters into a cup, when an axelaxe with frills flared burst into the 2-Eas lounge and called out, "We've got them!"

The counter seemed to fall from Brruuh's hand in slow motion. He launched himself across the table with no regard for the game setup.

In the loading bay of the 2-Eas, a space designed to bring aboard even the largest piece of mech replacement, a hoard of wrexi writhed like a single entity. A thousand pale-scaled lizards of similar builds and sizes. But Brruuh didn't need to pick out his wrexi, he could follow the ouaeahhn slipping through the crowd the way they piloted the ship through space, dodging movements as if they had some kind of notice it was about to happen.

And then there was a wrexi leaping into their arms. His wrexi. Sauraxen.

When he reached his mate, wrapped around the person with whom she was unbreakably bonded,

Sauraxen lifted her head. She reached out her hands, grabbing Brruuh even as her legs stayed locked around Matter's waist.

He took hold of her hand and found himself colliding with Matter's back.

Matter and Sauraxen's scents had been interwoven since that first day on Galactic Whale when they had embraced just like this, all Sauraxen's sensory hair wrapping around Matter like limbs. Even now, after days apart, there was still an underlying connection clear to Brruuh's senses. He'd thought it was based in the casual contact they shared, but it was more akin to the way Basti and Dimae's scents were mingled. More permanent.

It should have bothered him. Dimae once said if Basti spent too much time with Matter, enough to change either of their scents, Dimae's jealousy reared its head. Harrushetti culture stated that sharing clothes with someone's mate was trying to steal them out from under them. But with Matter and Sauraxen it didn't do anything to Brruuh. His indifference confused him, almost bothered him in itself, but he had never known Sauraxen without Matter, they came as a package deal.

But now, in the wake of fraught emotions and with his chest pressed tight to Matter's back, vision tinted with their sparkling array of colours, Brruuh realised that maybe it wasn't just that Sauraxen came with Matter as a packaged deal, it was that Brruuh wanted to be part of that package.

How could that be? Harrushetti were hyper-monogamous. He didn't have the biological capacity for that, to love more than one person in a romantic and exclusive way. But what if he did? Because of his adolescence alone or even just because he was Brruuh: individual not Brruuh: harrushetti avatar. Did it matter why? Or did it only matter that he tried to be honest with himself and the people he loved? His Ahthae?

"Let's go home," he whispered.

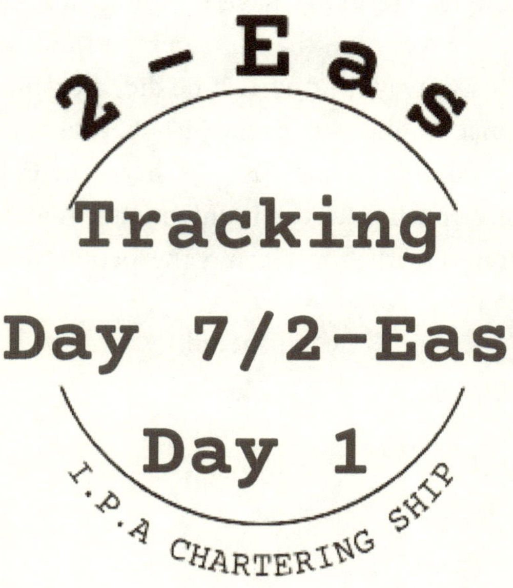

Dimae

Dimae understood, from a medical perspective, why he wasn't allowed to run straight to Galactic Whale and find his Bond Mate. He would inevitably not have let his patient run off like that either. But having to go to the rescue ships medi-centre, having to stay there after seeing Sauraxen scooped up by the other Galactic Whale crew. Having to sit and wait instead of immediately finding Basti hurt in a way Dimae couldn't describe.

But the night had passed and Dimae was, for the

most part, fine and so he got himself dismissed to head home. A vessel the size of the 2-Eas had a landing bay for smaller ships like Galactic Whale when they needed rescue or containment.

The space gunk had been cleaned off the exterior of his home ship, revealing a bright red exterior all neat and new-looking, the atmospheric thrusters dotted all over the surface in little black spots. Cleaner than Dimae had ever seen it. He'd assumed it would be the same silver that the scraped off name plate had ended up, but apparently that wasn't the case. He made his way up the still rattling boarding plank, up the gravity well, and into the aufenthaltsraum where the scent of Basti lead him.

Basti burst to his feet, stumbling forward to wrap his arms around Dimae. And something in Dimae settled, like all of his fur had been stood on end and now lay flat.

The tang of sulphur clung to Basti, distorting his scent even as Dimae pressed his nose tight into the juncture of his bond mate's neck and shoulder. Salt stung the air as tears seeped into Dimae's fur. The precious contact broke when Basti leaned away to cough.

"How long were you on the surface of Pitzk?" Dimae demanded when the coughing abated.

"Long enough to find the ship, but the sulphur leaked down into the tunnel Sau and I were trapped in too."

"How long?"

"Maybe a few hours. I got everyone decontaminated when we made it back here."

Oh. He thought Dimae was mad at him instead of desperate and professional. Dimae pressed a kiss to the top of his head, between where his ears should have been if he was a harrushetti. "You did wonderfully. Come to medi-bay with me."

Basti groaned, body slumping in Dimae's grip. But he tensed and coughing overtook him again. Dimae waited for it to pass before leading Basti down the gravity well and into his domain.

"You're so ridiculous," Basti teased as he sat on the examination bed. "I only just got you back and your first instinct is to drag me back to work?"

From anyone else, in another other tone of voice, that might have been mocking. Or a legitimate complaint. From Basti, though, and with the smile affixed to his tempting mouth, it was indulgent. Proof of love deeper than the most vast ice caverns on Harrush.

Dimae rubbed his face against the stubble on Basti's jaw then turned back to his cupboards, untouched since disembarking to Pitzk. Of course, he'd prepared the medicine to ward against the atmospheric sulphur in his travel medi-pak but that was in some collection of items on the 2-Eas somewhere. Luck held that he had extras of all the required medicine. Not luck, exactly, more Dimae's over-preparedness. Which meant no need to emerge from his domain. No need to face the reality of what he had been through just yet.

"What are you about to put me through?" Basti asked, trepidation creeping in.

"Nei needles," Dimae promised. "I just have a theory." A theory he had begun developing on Pitzk to maybe treat Sau—whether it would be a cure or just a softening of symptoms was yet to be ascertained. The thought had been ticking over in his mind as he treated wrexi after wrexi, watching the way they got less vibrant in the poorly filtered recycled air. Air recycling wasn't a problem for Sauraxen on Galactic Whale, but even Dimae could taste the staleness of what they were breathing in that cargo bay.

"If I'm going to be your guinea pig just now, I expect full recompense."

Dimae tilted his head at Basti.

"A guinea pig in this context is a creature to be experimented on. And my recompense is a reference to wanting to make love."

Dimae's ears flicked as if someone else might have heard. Never mind that they were alone on the ship.

"I'm all but extorting sexual favours out of you." He trailed his eyes up Dimae's body performatively.

Dimae huffed a laugh. "After."

"Promises promises."

Brruuh

"I owe you an apology." The words were tentative, quiet so as not to disturb the wrexi that shifted around outside and inside medi-bay on the 2-Eas. Matter had been unceremoniously ousted from the room and Brruuh had taken Sauraxen's gesture to follow them. She'd only agreed to venture into medi-bay under protest after Matter and Brruuh had noticed the blood staining her fingers and wrist.

Brruuh's ears twitched but he said nothing in response. What could he say? That Matter did owe him an apology? That he owed them one in kind? That he understood they were both functioning under stress? That maybe he had been so hurt by the discovery because it made him question feelings he hadn't even known about at the time?

"What I said was unreasonable," Matter continued. "I don't really believe you would only offer contact for the purpose of keeping me alive, because it's your job or your duty. I got all tangled up in feeling like your cultural boundaries were being broken and being defensive about my medical shit."

"It was inappropriate for me to take the position I

took, also," Brruuh said. "I was afraid."

"But we got her back, just like I said we would."

That wasn't what he had been afraid of. But before Brruuh could start speaking further about those feelings or his recent attempts to interpret them, a wrexi wrapped arms and legs and sensory hair around Matter from behind.

They let out a little oof and then beamed. "Lacha?"

"Matter!"

Matter gripped the arms around their torso and squeezed lightly.

A growl placed itself in Brruuh's chest but he swallowed it. What was he growling for? Being interrupted? Because Lacha had wrapped themself around Matter? It hadn't been a problem when Sauraxen did it and it was Sauraxen he was supposed to be bonding—or bonded with. And he'd seen how close Matter and Lacha had got on Pitzk, why was it a problem now?

"I'd ask how you are but that seems a ridiculous question," Matter said.

"I'm uninjured."

Matter let out a silly little whoop. "Then what are you doing in medi-bay?"

"These doctors want to check me over before they're convinced I'm fine. As if I don't know my own body."

"Ugh, doctors, am I right? Tell you what, let's just blow them off—idiom—and go hang out in the aufenthaltsraum of this ship."

"It's a lounge here," Brruuh corrected.

"Fancy," Matter joked to him. "Will you tell Sauraxen where I am?"

Brruuh nodded. The desire to rail at them about how they could possibly leave Sauraxen in a situation like this to spend time with someone else solidified in his chest like ice. But he held it in. Not only did he not want to panic these poor wrexi around him who had already been through so much, but Matter had just swallowed their pride to apologise to him. And, even if they hadn't, he could hardly hold them to his own cultural or personal standards.

But he couldn't understand it. How was Sauraxen not the most important person to come back to them both?

He didn't have to wait much longer for Sauraxen to emerge from medi-bay. "Where's Matter?" she asked.

"In the lounge with Lacha."

Sauraxen tipped her chin back in a wrexi smile. "Get you all to myself for a bit. Or do you want to go hang out with them?"

Brruuh shook his head.

Sauraxen's smile faltered. "Did something happen?"

"Nei," Brruuh lied. "I just like spending time alone with you."

"That was practically saucy coming from you."

Matter

The 2-Eas lounge was shockingly comfortable with sofas like beanbags dotted around the space. A huge game table took up a generous portion of space, with access to other types of game pieces stashed in clear cupboards along the walls. Above their heads a huge dome showed the glittering expanse of space—a view Lacha no doubt couldn't take in with her wrexi-perception. Not that is was much of a view with the trafficking ship parked directly in front of it.

Matter crashed down onto one of the soft sofas with Lacha, snuggling close to the wrexi and turning away from the void for the first time in their life.

"What do you think they're going to do?" Lacha asked.

"What do you mean?"

"About the ship? About all of us?"

"I guess we'll find out... I know the chief of security here so I can ask," Matter offered.

Lacha nodded against them.

"Oh, now?"

"Is that okay?"

"Sure." Matter shifted to pull up communications

on their wristband and typed out a quick message to Benoit.

It seemed like no time had passed before the pahrushi appeared, Ezeks at his back—though the lounge had filled up somewhat with 2-Eas crew, living and playing in their relaxation area, all but ignoring the pair of interlopers where they had set themselves up—so maybe it had been a while and Matter just hadn't noticed.

Benoit settled himself on the sofa, close but not touching them, crossing his legs beneath him and letting his wings rest against the soft cushions. "The ship was effectively gutted," he said. "It's incapable of flying, but we're going to take some extra precautions and let our engineers take out the necessary pieces to ensure they can't fix it. We're going to tractor it until an IPA station or ship with more appropriate tools can come and get it. And in the meantime, we're going to take all the wrexi who want to go back to Pitzk. We're going to remain there until an IPA border patrol vessel can come and set up better security and repairs as necessary. And we've put in a request—"

"Demand," Ezeks corrected.

"For improved communications with the planet." He looked at Matter, grief and apologies plastered across his face.

"It's not your fault this happened," Matter reassured. "It's not any of our faults."

"I'm the one who left the service designed to

prevent this kind of thing," Benoit huffed. "I'm the one—"

He didn't need to finish his sentence, though, Matter heard it well enough. I'm the one who knows about it. I'm the one who has the skills. I'm the one who can fix it. If I just let myself get hurt a little then everybody else can be safe.

Benoit met their gaze, flinching when he saw himself reflected there.

Matter leaned a little heavier on Lacha. "Does that help?"

"It should," the wrexi muttered.

"I get it."

"Oh?"

"I've been where you are." Kidnapped. Trafficked. Hurt.

Lacha snuggled closer. The sofa shifted as Ezeks moved to join them both, xyr soothing wash of tele-empathic care settling like a blanket over the pair of them. Benoit stood, hesitated, and left the lounge.

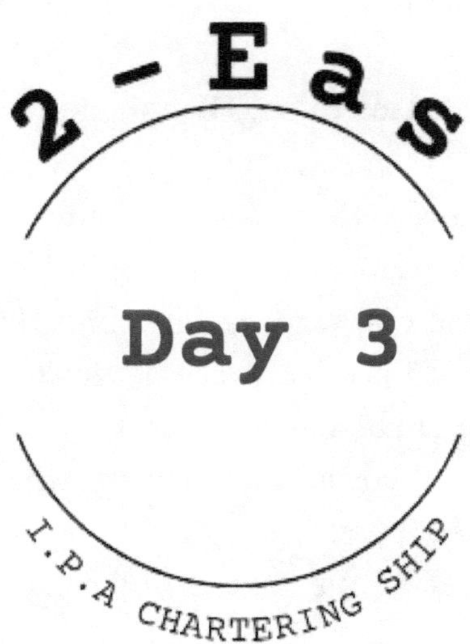

Brruuh

Brruuh announced his presence with a soft rumble before he stepped into medi-bay. Dimae had been back for a few days and was already hard at work, at least for short periods of time. Brruuh on the other hand hadn't been able to tear himself away from Sauraxen at all until she insisted on dipping into Galactic Whale's engine rooms and told him he couldn't come or he'd distract her. Matter hadn't made it back to the ship, perhaps still in the 2-Eas lounge or wherever else they'd been spending their time aboard.

Two crates stamped with the 2-Eas ship registration sat in the centre of medi-bay, the diagnostic bed pushed up against the wall so they could sit in its usual spot.

"Delivery?" Brruuh asked when Dimae offered his

attention.

"Medicine to replenish our stock," Dimae explained. "Are you well?"

"I have a problem but I'm not sure if it's medical or cultural."

Dimae gestured to the medical bed.

Brruuh hopped up to sit on it and let Dimae start basic scans.

"Tell me what's happening."

"I..." Brruuh trailed off. How did one go about explaining what he had been feeling? Jealousy and not-jealousy? That wouldn't make any sense. He touched a hand over his emotional centre, the swirling mass that had taken up residence there and switched to Earth Common Eurean, because harrushetti had no words for what he was experiencing. "It feels like my heart is being ripped in two."

Dimae's ears twitched forward, concerned meep escaping him.

"Not like that," Brruuh switched back to harrushetti. Reassuring Dimae that Sauraxen hadn't broken his heart, hadn't thrown him into heartbreak shock. "It's like one piece of it lies here." He held out a fist.

Dimae nodded.

"And there is another piece." He held out his other fist, separate from the first. "Here. But I don't have two. In order for it to be spilt it must have..." He clamped his hands together and slowly ripped them apart.

Dimae tilted his head. "Explain where the pieces are."

Brruuh's ears dipped back, his shoulders hunched and he tried not to squirm like a kitten. He hadn't thought he would experience the awful embarrassment of explaining his feelings to an authority figure like a riarch. But Dimae was his captain's husband, and that put him in a position of authority. He had to admit, there was a certain amount of nostalgia in that.

He took a breath. He was a professional cognitivist. Explaining feelings was his life's work. Not to mention he was a fully formed adult and, while Dimae might be in his Ahthae—his chosen and only family—and hold a position of authority, he was not, in fact a riarch to be faced and placated. Brruuh was asking a friend for advice. He could do this. "One piece lies with my court-mate." As it should. As his whole heart should really.

"And the other?"

"Elsewhere," Brruuh hedged.

Dimae offered only a flat look.

"With someone else."

"And you're certain these two feelings are the same."

"Not the same." His feelings for Sauraxen had started with interest, had built in humour and solidified in care. That was still the foundation and function of their relationship, the tenets by which it existed and the soft new colour that had developed in it. Sauraxen shone like the heart of Harrush and loving her felt like being home for the first time since the flood. It was how Brruuh had always imagined love would be.

His other feelings had been hidden, or ignored. More subtle until they suddenly crashed over him in a shock of realisation that he didn't know what to do with. Impossible to untangle when exactly they started, how they had come to exist the way they did now. Like a swirling gravitational orbit he hadn't noticed he got caught in.

"If it doesn't feel the same, maybe it isn't," Dimae suggested. "You could be misinterpreting your body's signals. Or it's a familial bond. Or some new sort of friendship." He paused, ears flicking tentatively. "It's not...?"

"It's not your Bond Mate, don't worry."

Dimae trilled an apology.

"Matter makes everyone feel at home," Dimae muttered. Because of course he could figure out to whom Brruuh's heart had taken its wandering. If it wasn't Basti, and he was coming to Dimae for assistance with it, who else could these feelings possibly be focused toward? "It's just Ahthae."

Brruuh started to argue that it felt different. That arguing with Matter held the thrill of a dance that used to be a fight. That there was something in them that called to the wilder more instinctive parts of him that wanted to be protected. But he closed his mouth and hopped down from the bed. "As long as I'm not broken."

Dimae made a confirming noise and Brruuh scuttled from the room and straight to engineering.

Sauraxen emerged from the shadows and immediately ran a hand down his arm. A wrexi gesture he had already taken to.

"I need to talk to you," he blurted.

"Seems serious, can I finish what I was doing?"

No. He needed to ease the fear that he had broken her heart the same way as her ex. "Ja," he said instead. "Come up to my office when you're done?"

"I had plans with Matter later."

Brruuh's ears pressed flat against his head. "It can wait," he said, not sure if it was a lie.

Matter

According to Ezeks, the huge lounge window wasn't always open to allow the view of space because it could make people dizzy, but Sauraxen, Matter, Ezeks, and Lacha lay together on one of the huge sofas staring into the void—as much as Sauraxen and Lacha could possibly be staring anywhere—and just existing together.

"You're better with her," Ezeks whispered into Matter's mind.

They nodded, leaning down so their chin rested atop Sauraxen's head. She hadn't said anything about her time aboard the kidnaping ship, but she also hadn't spent any time with the wrexi who now roamed around the 2-Eas—with the current exception of Lacha. And, of course, Sau, who had taken up a space in one of the unused crew quarters on Galactic Whale.

Matter wasn't about to ask. They had their own trauma to bring to this pity party.

Staring up at the stars with the comfort bodies pressed around them seemed to have tinted the trails purple and blue. Unless... "What is that?"

"What?" Ezeks asked.

"Purple thing?"

"I don't see anything," Lacha huffed.

"Ouaeahhn sight," Sauraxen explained. "What does it look like?"

"It's moving pretty fast. Faster than something that size should..." They surge off the sofa. "Oh fuck!"

"What? What's wrong?" All three of their companions had also scrambled up.

"We're about to get dumped on Ouaeahhn."

"What?" Ezeks asked as Sauraxen jumped in with "Why?"

"IPA rules state we drop you off at the nearest planet or station able to deal with your technically-illegal movements," Ezeks explained. "And take the rest of the wrexi either back to Pitzk or to another ship more capable of hosting such a large group of refugees."

"We have to go back?" Lacha asked.

"Technically you can apply for residency in another IPA zone," Sauraxen argued. "Which is kind of complicated but entirely within your rights."

"But the point right now" Ezeks interrupted before she could get going, "is what do you mean it's Ouaeahhn?"

"Ouaeahhn is a trans-orbital asteroid with planetary status," Matter explained. "It moves through space without a fixed orbit and… well, it's right there." They pointed through the glass to where the awkward-sized purple planet had appeared, caught up in the nearest star's orbit, at least for now.

"We need to find Brruuh and Basti," Sauraxen declared. "Our deadline just got crunched."

"I…" Matter looked at Ezeks, something like longing swelling within them. "I'll meet you on the ship," they told Sauraxen.

She scurried off.

"You're not going with her?" Ezeks asked.

"Can't leave without saying goodbye."

"I know it was a traumatic time for you, but it was really nice having another tele-empath on board."

"Same. I can't begin to—"

"Don't thank me," Ezeks interrupted. "It's rude in axelaxe culture. Just keep in touch. I need you to keep feeding me your captain's favourite classic earth vids—they're wacky."

Matter laughed.

They turned to Lacha, who shook their head. "Nei. Don't say goodbye."

Matter closed their mouth.

Lacha swapped to wrexi. "Follow another tunnel, they all come to meet."

"Anouniea," Matter answered in ouaeahhn, thanking both of them for helping to fix the broken feeling they'd been carting around.

"Wait," Ezeks called. "Here." Xe slipped xyr own personal shields off xyr wrist and onto Matter's. It was an axelaxe made one, woven to work both in and out of water, green and pink where Matter's had always been purple. "I'll get another when I can, but if you're going to Ouaeahhn, you're going to need this."

Sebastian

Sauraxen burst into the captain's quarters without knocking. Basti's mouth was open to remind her that humans and harrushetti liked their privacy, especially since he and Dimae were currently in their nest and completely naked and busy. And, more importantly, Sauraxen had agreed to abide by human style privacy guidelines. But before he could get any of that out she was speaking, "It's not two more weeks to the nearest IPA Station, it's now."

"How can it be now?"

"Ouaeahhn."

Basti leapt to his feet, wracked with coughing from moving too fast. He caught himself on the wall, pressing his other hand to his chest as if it would hold him together. Sauraxen waited, on the tips of her toes and bouncing slightly to mitigate her need to run.

"Get—" he wheezed "—everyone into the—"

"Aufenthaltsraum," she finished for him. "Got it." Then she had bolted back out of the room.

Basti sank down on the edge of the bed, trying to take deep breaths and feeling like he was drowning. Like his lungs were filled with seaweed and sticky algae.

Dimae rubbed a hand up and down his back in a smooth rhythm. "Is the medicine helping at all?"

Basti nodded and held out a hand. Dimae pressed the inhaler-like tube into his grip. When he started to hover, Basti waved him off.

By the time he got himself dressed and up to the aufenthaltsraum, the rest of the crew had already taken their places with steaming drinks in various receptacles placed in front of them. And Sau, sitting on the sofa with xyr own bowl of not-coffee. An honorary crew member as long as xe wanted to stay.

"We're about to land on Ouaeahhn," Basti said, though he had no doubt everyone had already been informed, since Brruuh and Sau were the only two who hadn't already known. "Which means we're going to face the reckoning for absconding from Gnarresh-Fle without waiting for permission."

"What do you need from us?" Brruuh asked.

"All we have to do is stick to the truth of it. We knew waiting for a response would take too long and it was a medical emergency."

"What about the trafficking ship?" Matter asked.

"What about it? Two of our crew were kidnapped and we had an ouaeahhn pilot who could trail that ship. That's the kind of thing even the harshest member of the IPA couldn't punish us for, right?" He looked over to Brruuh, whose ears flicked in that uncomfortable sort-of-shrug harrushetti did. Basti took a long drink of his coffee. "We'll cross that bridge as we come to it."

"What bridge?" Dimae asked.

"It's an idiom," Matter explained. "It means we'll deal with that potential problem if it presents itself."

"I thought the bridge idiom was about burning things," Sauraxen interrupted.

"That's a different bridge idiom." They paused. "There's also a combination of the pair of them idiom—but that's a malaphor, technically."

"Would it help or hinder you more if I stayed?" Sau asked. Xe had moved from the sofa over to Basti with footsteps so silent Basti hadn't noticed.

"What do you mean?" Basti asked, matching Sau's soft tone while the others devolved into talking about idioms. Again. He couldn't help but smile indulgently at them.

"If I stay, in my current state, does it help your claim of medical necessity? Or would it be better if I remained with the other wrexi and return to Pitzk?"

"You're welcome to stay, Sau. Like I said, you're here for as long as you want. I don't want this to be the thing that makes the choice for you. If you want to return to Pitzk, you should. If you want to stay with us, then you should do that. We can make it work either way."

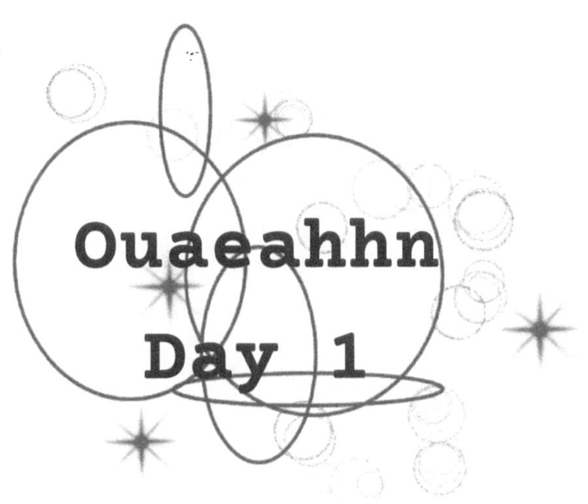

Sauraxen

There was a comfort to be found steering the ship out of the 2-Eas, even if it was just to land on Ouaeahhn. A comfort in leaving the rest of her people behind for the 2-Eas to return them back to Pitzk, where, in all hopefulness, an IPA planetary crew would be waiting to help repair what had been damaged by the traffickers.

Sauraxen might be 'of Pitzk' but that wasn't her home anymore. Getting back into the comfort of her little clunker, a thing that needed her skills to keep functioning couldn't have come soon enough. Even if it was only a little jump from ship to planet.

Ouaeahhn itself drew Sauraxen in like nowhere else had. Descending the boarding plank with Basti, Dimae, and her vava—who had opted to remain at least for now. Opted to spend xyr wasting out amongst the stars xe had never had the opportunity to explore before. When your priority was raising children, exploring the stars was an unlikely tunnel destination for you.

Ouaeahhn was Matter planetified. That glittering holographic, reflective nature with a little more purple. Light soft enough that even Sauraxen's eyes could make out the haze of it. The trees stretched up to the tip of the rippling shield where the atmosphere had, presumably, once been. A whole planet with a mechanically shielded atmosphere was like something out of Sauraxen's wildest imaginings. Would they let her into their shield mechanics? Probably not. But it would be worth asking.

Once she stepped foot on the planet's surface, the whole thing seemed to reverberate beneath her, as if the planet itself were trying to accommodate her needs. Unlike their arrival at Gnarresh-Fle—a cold and detached sort of place—a small welcoming party stood to greet them off the ship. Bright sweeping gestures sending the fabric draped over their bodies rippling. They offered food and drink, invited Sau and Sauraxen to settle in comfortable chair-beds that already felt like sinking into clouds before she had even tried them. She should have known Ouaeahhn would be like this, these people matched Matter's welcoming energy to such a degree that it would be impossible not to correlate them.

And yet… there was a notable lack of Matter on the planet. Even as she and her vava made their way through the little snack plate perched between them on the cloud—how that didn't spill Sauraxen couldn't imagine—Matter didn't appear. Far too long for simple post-flight checks.

Basti and Dimae had headed off with one of the ouaeahhn who wore a cuff around an arm to denote status within the IPA, letters raised so even Sauraxen could perceive the rank.

Brruuh was, notably, also absent.

"I could get used to this," vava muttered as the trees shifted once again to provide optimum shade where the pair of them sat. "Do you think they would let me stay?"

"What happened to exploring the stars?" Sauraxen teased.

"As far as I heard, this planet moves in space. I can see the stars just fine from this comfy bed."

Brruuh

He tapped sheathed claws on the edge of the pilot's console doorframe to announce his presence. A human habit he chose for this situation since it would likely put Matter more at ease than a harrushetti greeting.

Out of the dome, the planet—trans-orbital asteroid—of Ouaeahhn spread out like a haze of purple, a mirage in the deepest void of space. Even through the window, Matter should have matched it, the way their holographic skin and eyes reflected colours back. Their hair more purple than anything else. But, whether by the black block of their jumpsuit, or some other disconnect, they didn't fit.

Brruuh's ears drew back. The melancholy they stared down at the planet with, the resistance, it was how he felt on Harrush. The conflicted nature of being in a home that no longer felt the way it once had. That, perhaps, no longer felt like a home at all.

He took a deep breath, the air filling his lungs entirely consumed by the scent of Matter.

"I'm going to stay on the ship, you might as well go down," Matter announced, staring out the dome.

"Oh?" Brruuh asked, carefully neutral. He leaned against the door frame, aiming for something casual. Fearing he fell short.

"It's a tele-empathic planet, it's not fair to invite the whole thing: people, plants, trees, animals, everything else into my pain with me."

He let out a quiet hum.

"I've seen what it does to people. Even you, when you only got a blip of it. It's overwhelming. People cry, they scream, they fall to the ground and writhe around in pain."

"And that's what you live with?" The concept was horrifying, he had to clamp down on his secondary vocal cords to keep them from voicing his emotions. It wasn't fair to be horrified. Not now.

"I'm used to it."

Brruuh fiddled with his claws, extending and retracting them in time with his breaths. "Do you want to go to the ground?"

Matter finally turned to him, all wide eyes. Hope and fear warring within them as they reflected his own grey stripes back at him.

"You're just afraid of hurting people?"

They nodded slowly.

Brruuh held out a hand. Matter unfolded from the pilot's chair but didn't take it yet. "I won't let you."

"What do you mean?"

"I mean, if you remain in contact with me, my harrushetti blocking will likely mediate it. I will bring you back if you begin causing damage. And I will stay with you either way."

"You promise?"

"I promise."

They took his offered hand and let Brruuh walk

them off the ship. He had done it for an IPA fugitive once, walked them to a cognitive assessment session. It had been very different from this except for the stiff, fear-filled body beside him. The scent a sickly sweet thing that curled around him in a tight embrace, sinking into his lungs and playing with the sensitive hairs in his ears.

They both paused at the edge of the boarding plank, just inside the ship's shields. The planet beyond shone and glittered that same holographic sparkle as Matter on their best day. Matter with Lacha and Ezeks and Sauraxen, and seemingly never with Brruuh.

"I promise," Brruuh reiterated in a whisper.

Matter toed off their untied boots and stepped onto the purple ground of Ouaeahhn.

"Ahni?" someone shouted, the word echoing weirdly in Brruuh's head as well as his ears. They bounded over and wrapped Matter up in a hug so boisterous that Brruuh almost let go of Matter's hand.

"La-al," Matter breathed as the hug settled and separated.

La-al lunged toward Brruuh and collided with Matter instead as they jerked in front of him, face twisting that way it did when movement reminded them previously ignored pain existed.

"He doesn't hug," Matter explained.

"Oh," La-al sighed. Tall but otherwise built like Matter, La-al had more of a swirling cosmos playing out over skin a little darker than Matter's. Hair in loose waves hung long over shoulders, the colour melding with the woven pattern of the clothing shrouding the body beneath in some level of mystery. Not that Brruuh wasn't aware of limb placement and makeup based on his experience with Matter and Hnan amongst other ouaeahhn he'd met. La-al brightened quickly, turning a blinding smile onto Brruuh. "I'm Laalttrnuou."

"La-al-tt-ru-nou?" Brruuh echoed, knowing it wasn't quite right. That ending had more layers to it than he managed. New-ew instead of nou.

"It means falling stars and collaborative work. But you can call me La-al, everybody does."

"I'm Brruuh, it means playful."

"It does?" Matter asked.

Brruuh's ears dropped, he hadn't meant to share that part.

"Ah," Matter laughed, "the free-fall got you."

"The what?"

"La-al, free-fall and gravity. She pulls you to reveal things unintentionally. It gets the best of all of us."

"And how are you at making home moving through the stars, Ymmattrahni?" La-al snarked.

"They're good at it," Brruuh answered. "But I heard their name can also mean homewrecker."

"Not with its intended tele-empathic signature. Oh, but you can't feel those, can you?"

Brruuh shook his head.

"It would be a very cruel translation. Ymmattrahni breaks down into Ym—potential for danger, and ma—movement. Then ah—home or family and ni—feeling. So you can see how someone might choose to misinterpret it as moving between homes and breaking the feeling of family."

Brruuh nodded.

"But, I have to ask, knowing Ahni here, would you put those things together to mean that?"

"Of course not," Brruuh said easily. "Matter feels like home, they built me a family I never thought I would find." His eyes narrowed. "Desist free-falling me."

La-al's laugh was musical. "You building a bigger and bigger Ahthae?" she asked Matter.

"Always." Matter's eyes crinkled at the corners when they smiled in the same way Basti's did.

"And he doesn't hug?" La-al asked, head tilting to one side.

"A hug is reserved only for those I am closest to," Brruuh explained.

"That's actually kinda beautiful," La-al said. "Weird, but beautiful. Anyway, you want to come harvest sehn with me?"

"Sure," Matter agreed easily.

Brruuh trailed after them as they and La-al conversed in Ouaeahhn, the language melodic and sighing with some pieces lost to Brruuh's senses entirely by the telepathic element. The translator murmuring in his ear only providing the most overarching possible translation to each piece of word, leaving Brruuh stumbling for what those might turn into when paired together.

La-al led them both to a grove of trees, leaves of silver and purple shifting in a soft breeze that didn't seem to exist against Brruuh's skin. Brruuh expected it to look like harvesting he had seen before, reaching up and plucking fruit or leaves off the tree. Putting them into pockets or scooping up the bottom of the—would he call that a robe? It looked like a blanket tied at one shoulder—outfit La-al wore to create a basket. Instead, both Matter and La-al laid a hand on each tree and the trees themselves lowered and extended branches to weave into small baskets, shaking their loose leaves off in a sudden stronger breeze that similarly didn't exist.

"Do you want to try?" Matter asked Brruuh.

"I'm not..."

They shrugged a shoulder but their face shuttered a little, hurt spiking through the contact between them.

Brruuh reached out his free hand, touching the tree hesitantly. Matter's breath ghosted over his shoulder, their fingers warm in his. He closed his eyes, trying to ignore the way that contact—that closeness hummed against his fur. So similar to how being close to Sauraxen felt.

"Oh wow," La-al breathed.

Brruuh opened his eyes to find the grove of trees blooming with bright silver blossoms. The flowers rained down gently onto their heads and into the baskets Matter and La-al held. "What is that?" Brruuh asked, ear flicking as one landed against it and reaching out to catch another.

"That's you through ouaeahhn eyes," La-al answered.

He looked against at the glittering silver flower cradled in his paw. It reminded him of the way Matter reflected YaBin colours back to him. But that made sense, since it was him reflected through Matter's ouaeahhn eyes. Still, something about it made his emotional core squirm.

Matter's fingers squeezed his and Brruuh's ears flicked in embarrassment. Could they feel that through their bond? Hopefully not. He needed to speak with Sauraxen about it before Matter could ever be allowed to find out. And he still hadn't quite built himself up to manage such a feat yet, especially since they kept getting interrupted.

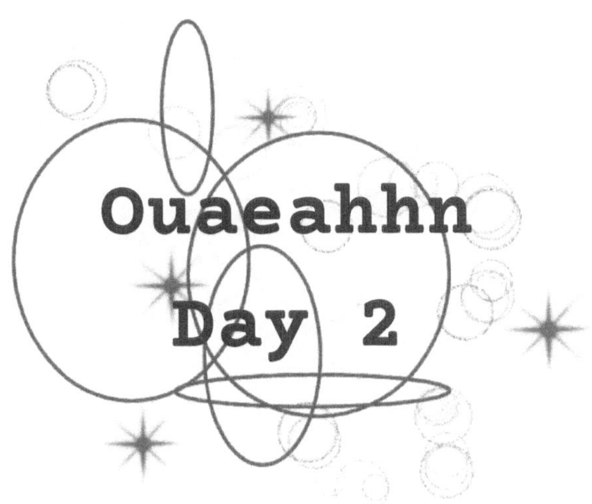

Ouaeahhn Day 2

Matter

They had decided to go back to the ship at night, not willing to risk letting other ouaeahhn into their dreams even with the safety offered by Ezeks' personal shields. It would hardly be fair to cling to Brruuh all night, both since harrushetti slept in bursts and because he would want to be with Sauraxen at least some of the time. And, weird as it might be to other ouaeahhn, Matter was used to being alone, they missed it when they spent a long time with other people. Even La-al was a little much in such a concentrated burst.

Which meant when Matter stumbled into the aufenthaltsraum the next morning in search of coffee and maybe breakfast, they expected to be alone. Instead, Sauraxen and Brruuh danced around each other with the smooth perfection only gained through practise of spending time together. Until Brruuh jerked around to meet Matter's attention.

"Ciao," they offered.

Brruuh rumbled a squeak.

"Are you okay? Was it too much yesterday?"

"It's not that," Brruuh admitted. He sighed heavily. "I need to talk to you both."

"Oh!" Sauraxen gasped, "I forgot to come see you when I said I would, with Ouaeahhn and everything…"

"Nei," Brruuh reassured. "I understand, things get in the way at times."

"What's wrong?" Matter asked, steering the conversation back to the matter at hand and wishing they could have got coffee first.

"This isn't working," Brruuh said bluntly.

"Are you breaking up with me in front of my best friend?" Sauraxen asked.

"What? Nei! Nei, I'm… It's…" He pulled out a chair and sank into it, burying his face in his hands. "I'm broken."

Matter looked at Sauraxen over his head. She minutely shook her head, no extra info to add.

"Broken how?" Matter asked.

"We're meant to be…Harrushetti are hyper-monogamous because of evolutionary things that I don't really understand. I'm neither a historian nor a medical professional, all I know is the way we bond with our chosen partner changes us, physically alters us in a way that lets us share each other's fortitude and warmth. It's why we die of heartbreak."

"Okay." Matter slid into a chair. "And you're saying…?"

"I am finding my heart in two places."

"You're in love with someone else?" Sauraxen asked. "Not instead but as well?"

Brruuh nodded morosely.

"That's fine," Sauraxen said with a laugh, laying herself over his shoulders in a strange and incredibly wrexi hug.

"But—"

"We can make a V."

Brruuh looked up, ears tilted forward in confusion.

"Where one person has two partners who aren't necessarily each other's partners," Matter explained. They formed a triangle on the dining table out of the trio of mugs there. They put a spoon pointing outwards from the Brruuh mug to Sauraxen's bowl-mug and another to the third mug. Was that coffee? Had someone prepared that for Matter? "You'd be the centre of the V with a branch for each paramour."

"I don't…"

"It's okay if you don't know how to do that," Matter continued. "It's different for everyone. You figure it out with the people involved and work from there. Why are you looking at me like I'm missing something vital?"

"I don't want that. I don't want—" his secondary vocal cords rumbled, filling the room and cutting off his own sentence. He dragged the mugs together into a huddle.

Matter tilted their head. "People would potentially agree to that." But who in the void was he asking? Because the other wrexi had all wandered off with the 2-Eas so it was a bit late to ask them. And the only person he'd met on Ouaeahhn so far was La-al.

"I felt like I was dying when you went off with the axelaxe."

"Ezeks? Why?"

"Oh," Sauraxen gasped.

Brruuh pushed to his feet and stalked toward Matter. Leaning over them, he caught himself with one hand on the back of their chair.

Matter tilted their head at him.

"We could be a triad," Sauraxen suggested. "You, me, and Matter. That's what you're trying to say, right?"

Brruuh nodded.

"What?" Matter asked. "Whoa, wait, what?"

Brruuh's nose trailed over their head, ruffling hair not yet pulled into the usual space buns.

"But you and I aren't even..." Matter trailed off, looking at Sauraxen with a level of desperation. "And I don't really feel romantic attraction..."

"You said yourself that every relationship works

with what the people inside it want," Sauraxen said.

"Why are you on his side!?" Matter shoved back, sliding awkwardly out of the chair and falling onto the floor of the aufenthaltsraum.

"I'm on my own side," Sauraxen explained.

"Are you trying to tell me you've been harbouring *feelings* for me?"

"Nei, but this way everyone gets to be happy, right? You and I can be together like we used to be, friends with benefits. Brruuh and I can be together with all that romance and stuff. And you and Brruuh can be together and figure out how that looks for you two, nei romance required."

Brruuh offered a calm hand, some of the intensity dissolved in the face of Matter's abject panic. They let him help them up but he held on after they were sturdy on their feet, examining the new Ounu decorating their hand from their wrist to the base of their thumb. "This is new."

"Ja, they happen, remember?"

"You said it was formative experiences."

"It is. When I was with Lacha on Pitzk—" Brruuh tossed his own hands into the air and stalked away. "See this is part of it, I need contact to survive, I can't just—"

"Meaningful contact," Brruuh interrupted.

"Ja, okay, meaningful contact. But I need to be able to access that regardless of your feelings or accessibility."

"I understand you're a contactey person—"

"And I don't get to decide when ounu happens. It's not like a tattoo. I didn't get to choose to have remnants of the worst experience of my life littered across my torso."

"Then this is a bad thing?"

"Nei." Matter ran their fingers across the raised scale-like pattern on their hand. The highest points of it shone with that Pitzki-mushroom blue that Lacha had painted down their sides. The tele-empathic focus filled Matter with that sense of understanding and care.

"Is that why it always feels so…?" Sauraxen started to ask but trailed off.

Matter shrugged, folding their arms around themself. Tele-empathic markings definitely made people feel a certain way.

"Equally, I do not control the feelings I have," Brruuh huffed.

"So what then? We form this bond and I risk hurting you every time I need contact? Or every time I *want* to have contact? Or when I get new ounu? It's not like I don't care about you, Brruuh, I don't exactly relish the thought of putting you through that for things I can't change."

Brruuh huffed out a breath. "The trouble is that I didn't recognise my feelings quickly enough. When my feelings for Sauraxen first began, I told her, to open up the opportunity for rejection before it became too much."

"You're trying to tell me that rejecting this attempted proposal might kill you?"

"Nei. Maybe. That's not what I'm—"

"How long have you felt this way?"

"I couldn't calculate for certain."

"Brruuh." No patience left, Matter's voice came out snappy.

"The whale changed things. You waking me up from near death changed things. But I didn't realise until we argued on the 2-Eas."

"Death by a thousand cuts," Matter mused, clarifying immediately with, "it's an idiom," lest Brruuh think any of them was about to die.

"Okay, tell me this," Sauraxen said. "Would adding Matter in change who is the cloak bearer and who is the dancer?"

The what?

"Nei, what we have would remain mostly consistent, I think."

"I can't believe you realised how you felt about me from an argument," Matter huffed.

"Harrushetti courting has always involved an element of danger."

Dimae

"**I** have decided to remain here," Sau said, leaning back on the chair-bed and letting Dimae scan xem after inhaling the wash of medicine that emerged from the atomiser all over xyr sensory skin and hair. "My axen doesn't need her vava hanging around and it's nice here. They say it moves so I still get to explore space, experience things I never could have imagined."

"You don't have to," Dimae said. "You're welcome to remain with us as long as you like."

"I know. And I appreciate that. But here is… It's what Pitzk could be if we weren't constantly being hunted."

Dimae hummed. Discomfort twinged inside him. Would the IPA start fixing that problem—something that had apparently been going on far longer than Dimae could begin to excuse? Or would they just let it continue?

"There are worse places to die than this little asteroid where the trees make shade for me everywhere I go."

"I have news on that front, actually," Dimae said, trying to keep his kittenish impulses to a minimum as excitement thrummed through him. His scanner noting the changes in Sau from the absorption of the medicine. "You probably aren't going to die. At least not from this wasting."

Sau jerked up. "What?"

"I began this treatment for you based on treating the damage to Basti's lungs. Pitzki sulphur is adhesive, but it doesn't just adhere to your outsides, it adheres to your insides. For Basti it had clogged his lungs and was making it harder and harder to breathe. So I modified the protective medicine we use for the surface, added a piece to remove its adhesive quality, and some other lung-based medicines for humans." Like asthma meds, kept on hand for the worst cases that couldn't be cursed with early intervention, or sudden onset cases that needed stabilisation before they could use the curing tech. "I extrapolated how to adapt it for wrexi. I wasn't sure how it would function for you but my scans are coming back with improvement."

"The wasting is… over?"

"Pretty much. And I can send all the information to Pitzk and anywhere else inside the IPA, meaning everybody can access treatment."

"You figured out how to cure the oldest disease known to my culture?"

Dimae nodded, holding out the atomiser to Sau. "You'll need to keep taking the medicine for a while. Possibly forever but…"

Sau took the device in soft, cautious hands, as if worried that breaking or spilling it would destroy all the research as well. "You…I can't believe you fixed it."

Dimae settled himself on one of the other chair-beds. "We can't hope to heal everything. I didn't go in aiming for a cure. I was looking to help. To make it less bad. Matter taught me that not everything can be fixed and focusing only on cure hurts people in the long run. Treatment and care has to be the priority. Longevity matters more than cure. Happiness matters more than even that. But I don't know much about wrexi biology. When Basti presented symptoms it opened up my area of expertise. Human biology, human medicine is my best area of knowledge. And humans are hardy, they keep going in the face of impossible odds. Wrexi are a lot like that too." He slow-blinked, even knowing it would mean nothing to the people around him. "If you keep taking the medicine and aiming for healthy, you should get there."

Sau laughed. "You're doing the hatchling babble. I'm so grateful. I have nei words for it and I know you don't like physical contact so I won't try to hug you but hear this from me, Dr Dimae LeaYaPar-Jones, you gave me more life!"

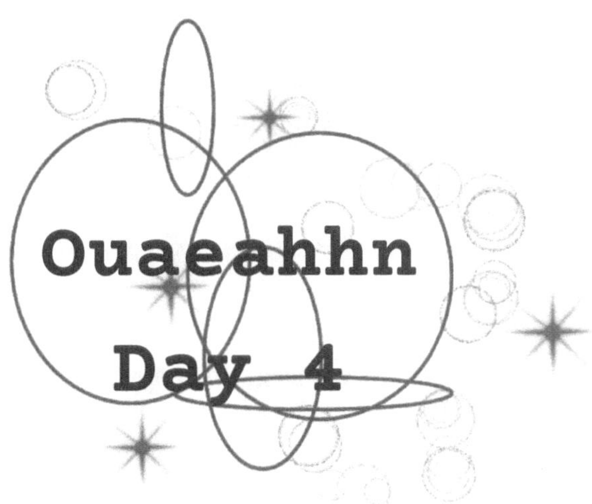

Sebastian

It took three days of requests to get into the meeting about everything that had happened. Three days of turning up at an ouaeahhn office building—as weird as it was to have an ouaeahhn office building when so little else seemed to have walls—and asking to be seen only to be informed over and over that the supervisory officer was off planet dealing with the orbiting shield management systems, and couldn't see him right now. To be asked to await the tele-empathic ping and have to explain that he wouldn't be able to feel a tele-empathic ping because he was human.

But finally, here he was, sat on what appeared to be a living tree branch in an office that was really just a wooden cavern, almost like a wasp nest but with an ouaeahhn bureaucrat instead of a wasp inside. Like every other planetary ouaeahhn Basti had seen so far, this one was dressed in a single knotted piece of fabric. This fabric had been decorated with clouds and stars that rippled with every movement. And, as with other IPA representatives here, had an armband embroidered with ouaeahhn language Basti couldn't read.

The branch was comfy, though, adapting to suit his shape and cradle his lower back in a way that he wished other chairs could do these days. Age really did wear on you. Or maybe it was all those years having to stand next to a captain's chair, or fitting himself into someone else's captain's chair. Basti didn't even have a captain's chair.

The bureaucrat across from him, no desk between them this time, just a pad clutched in a hand, smiled. Probably feeling the comfort Basti felt. Or worse, hearing him thinking about how he wished other IPA chairs could be this adaptive. Could he get a set of adaptive chairs on Galactic Whale? Probably not yet, but it was certainly something to put on his list.

It was peaceful in this office, too. Little glowing flowers decorated the ceiling, casting a warm light over the whole room. The soft sparkle of shielding glittering between the branches that made it up.

Maybe that shielding was more to do with its peace than the warm lights. No planet-full of ouaeahhn thoughts and feelings trying to get into Basti's ill-fitting head.

"Tell me exactly what you're hoping for," the bureaucrat requested, ECE stilted but clear, sliding long fingers across a datapad, a little frown taking up space in a crease between their eyebrows. Was this person a they? Basti couldn't find any pronoun pins or armband or other IPA standardised mechanic to denote such things. It was probably a tele-empathic output that everyone else normally on the planet could tell. He was overthinking already.

"Human telepathic output is..." They paused. "A little overwhelming at times and these records are mangled by my staff's confusion. I apologise that nobody could help you sooner."

Basti took a deep breath, trying to steel himself, trying to be less overwhelming. "I'm not sure where to start."

"Wherever you like is fine, we can piece it together. But I know humans see time as very linear, so the beginning—as you see it—is also welcome."

"We had some... trouble during out Deep Space Travel assessment."

"I have that from the IPA servers, ja."

"So we were ordered to stand in and around Gnarresh-Fle and Harrush with a provisional status on our ship license." And all their personal licenses too. "But one of my crew had a family medical emergency on Pitzk, so we had to make the trip."

"I see. Go on."

"And then we sort-of-accidentally took down a people trafficking operation with the 2-Eas."

"Your cargo runner and an exploration vessel took down an entire smuggling ring?"

Basti rubbed at the back of his neck, sheepish, as heat flooded his face. "At least one ship of it."

"Very well." The ouaeahhn typed something into the datapad—though typing was a generous word for the swirling motions that made text Basti couldn't read appear on the screen. The same style as the text beneath Matter's name on their quarter's door sign. "Carry on."

"The 2-Eas escorted us here—as it were—because a higher up IPA member needed to decide what reprimands we might face for..." he trailed off, not wanting to use the word 'illegal'. Then again, with ouaeahhn telepathy, the bureaucrat across from him probably already knew. "Unlicensed travelling."

"Well, that's ridiculous."

"I'm... sorry?"

"Nei reprimands necessary, obviously. You were responding to an emergency superseded by another emergency. It's rare, but these things do happen." The bureaucrat huffed. "It's so frustrating when the IPA won't allow for exceptions. The amount of work I've had to put in making them accept ouaeahhn variable tele-empathy. And they still haven't figured it out." They swiped those long fingers over the screen with a speed Basti couldn't help but stare at. "You've clearly proven yourselves capable—more than capable of inter-galactic travel with nei injury caused. The 2-Eas, a chartering ship has partnered with you and had nei complaints about your conduct or quality. Provisional status removed. You're officially licensed to cart cargo wherever your little human heart desires, as long as you do so within IPA stipulations."

"Oh…" Just like that? All that stress and worry and fear of his little found family breaking apart gone in the blink of one ouaeahhn's eye? "Thank you."

"Of course you're also more than welcome to remain here as long as you like, but I get the impression you're all much like Ymmattrahni, if you sit too long your boredom starts getting you into trouble."

Basti couldn't help but smile at that. None of his crew were designed to live planetside long term. Except maybe Dimae, but he would rather be with Basti.

"Tell your father to come back and visit, or at least write every once in a while."

"You know my dad?"

"Of course. We made Matter together."

"You're Matter's mama?"

"Well… nei. Ouaeahhn gender and relationships are more complex than that. And, as far as I understand it, human children don't like to hear what their parents got up to. But—"

"I need to sit down."

They smiled again. "You are sat down."

Oh right.

"Perhaps you would prefer to return to your Ahthae for comfort. Although, by the sounds of it, Matter isn't going to be providing comfort for a little while yet."

"Are they okay?"

"Oh, it's not the anla. It's Al-thae."

"I don't know what that means."

"It's… ECE only has the word love for so many concepts. We have more."

"Like Ahthae?"

"Ja. For most forms of love, we add a prefix to the start of the familial we: thae. Ahthae: home we."

There was something in the introduction of these ouaeahhn words, maybe because the planet lounged under his feet, maybe because they were shielded in this office, maybe the unfiltered way the words came with no translator buzzing beneath, but they pulled to the surface of Basti's mind thoughts and memories and emotions. His ship's crew, and the scent of coffee.

"Hnthae: planetary we."

Rows of plants with bright red and green berries, the weight of humidity pressing against him, against muscles sore from hard labour. And the fresh bright taste of freshly ground coffee.

"Nuthae: what you and Matter and Peggy have—though we do not have such concept here."

Arguments that turned silly with wrestling for the best seat on the sofa or the last bite of dessert with Peggy as their dad looked on with a poorly held in sigh. Staring up at the stars with Matter while the world cooled around them. Snapped words turning to soft hugs and the knowledge that no fight was too big to recover from, not really. Not for them. "Siblings?"

"That's it."

"You made a whole new word just for siblings?"

"When Matter discovered they had some, ja. We rarely procreate outside other ouaeahhn so we never had cause before."

"Then what's al?"

"Al is something with the brightness of the stars. Something that shines more beautifully than you have ever seen before. Something you would do anything for. That does not diminish the love or connection you have with others. Matter was my Althae once, yours is your ship, La-al has bonding with new people." They laid a hand on Basti's arm. "Let them have a little time before you lift off? And feel free to stock up while you're here. We have uncomfortably shaped and sized IPA crates you can—oh, could you actually take those to the nearest reuse centre?"

"Of course." Basti stood from the wood-woven chair; it morphed back into the office beneath his feet when it was nei longer needed. Freaky.

He could stock up first; ouaeahhn shared everything for the benefit of those who came with an open heart and honest intentions. Maybe he could get them to share one of those cloud-chair things? Or more than one. And he and Dimae could spend some time together.

Then back to the ship and into the stars.

For News About Latest
Releases
Join The Mailing List At:
WillSoulsbyMcCreath.com

About The Author

It's pronounced "Souls-Bee-Muh-Kreth"
As a cosplayer, Table-Top Gaming nerd, and videogamer; fiction has been a staple of Will's life forever. They like to corrupt their friends into joining these pass-times, or at least reading their stories.
Obsessed with every way to tell a story and every possible use for one, Will had few choices other than becoming a writer. A little too nosy for their own good they like to invest their time fixing other people's problems, and when that doesn't work they hand out stories to make you feel better.

Turn The Page For A
Preview From Will's
Upcoming Urban
Fantasy Series
**Claretbury
Chronicles**

Claretbury Chronicles 1
Contents Subject To Change

The whine-clunk of post being delivered was a rare sound in Billie's life. More often than not it was leaflets from local businesses: estate agents promising they could sell or rent Billie's place for buckets and bundles of cash, the best deals from a chain supermarket Billie had never been to, or the offer of cheaper wifi—all things directed to 'the occupant', never to Billie themself. So the white paper envelope with their name stamped across the front was a surprise.

They pulled it out from where it had stuck, hung halfway through their letter box. Bank stuff all came online now, and Billie's amenities were all dealt with by the Guild so it could only be—Billie flicked the envelope over to reveal the otherwise incongruous wax seal decorated with an interwoven H and G: The Hunters Guild.

The unmistakable smoke-scent of magic filed the air when Billie broke the seal.

Like every other letter from the Hunters Guild, it was impersonally type-writered; letters smudged and uneven in a way that had, at first, been jarring. Was still jarring if Billie spent any amount of time interacting with the world outside the Guild in paper form. Computer printed text was always neatly perfect measured rows. No misaligned keys causing a random e to leap as if it were meant to sit with the stalk of an h. But the Guild used type-writers because they were more resistant to magic. Nothing worse than having to shill out extra cash fixing or replacing tech that didn't play well with unexpected magic. Which was probably why Billie's Guild-provided laptop hadn't been updated since they first started out, and why it sounded like an aircraft trying to take off at regular intervals nei matter how hard Billie worked to maintain it.

Billie tossed the letter onto the shitty dining table that filled far too much of the studio flat—Guild procured, of course. Both the flat and the terrible table. They suited each other in a weird ill-fitting way, suited Billie much the same: Guild procured and Guild managed. The same level of care applied to all three.

At any rate, they wouldn't have to deal with this particular shitty table much longer since the Guild needed them to move. Again.

So much for the promise that they'd be left to maintain a specific area of the country: a city or county. Some interference from other arktoi would have been expected, but Myles had said they could stay where they were a while. A while that had, apparently, ended.

And Billie had trusted that promise from Myles enough to get rid of their moving boxes. No way they'd be able to get more in a Guild-appropriate timeline.

Billie had been an active member of the Hunters Guild since their teenage years, when their natural arkte powers had manifested amongst the other horrors of puberty. Go figure that most magic manifested in the most significantly developmental periods of growth: toddler and teenager. Ironically, being an arkte was the least traumatising part of puberty. At least until the Guild had come to collect them. Then it had been 'off to boarding school' aka stuck in elite monster hunting training with the rest of the arktoi.

Unfortunately for Billie, the Guild was used to

picking up the precursors to arkte magics in infancy. They had a whole department actively scrying for newly developing arktoi. Between that and the fact that arktoi tended to come in a particular flavour of gender, Billie was a rare exception twice over. Exceptions, like monsters, had no place in the Guild.

Used to living with loving parents and traditional state schooling, Billie had chafed under the expectation, the pressure, and the rigid authority of Guild training. Their parenting team had always encouraged questions, encouraged Billie to see things in a nuanced way. The Guild, on the other hand, wanted everything in binary categories: good or bad, human or monster, alive or dead. Billie didn't work well in binaries.

Still, once training was over, Billie was good at the job. Now the oldest and longest serving arkte in years and one of the few to achieve Certified Hunter Status in addition to arkte status. Not that Myles, the impersonal but handwritten M at the base of every one of these type-writered letters, saw this longevity as a good thing. If he did, he wouldn't be sending them to yet another impossible to survive scenario.

Although, Billie had survived the last one.

Acknowledgements

I'll start with the originator of my love of books, the woman who was endlessly willing to listen to stories as a kid, teen, and then adult figured out the pieces that are required to create novels. Mum, thanks for still being on my side. Dyslexia translator extraordinaire.
To my friends, longstanding and new, my Ahthae and my lifeline. It can be fraught existing in this world the way I do, I appreciate every single one of you who treats me like a normal person, and especially those who had offered refuge should I need it.
To my online friends, Tumblr mutuals, WordPress commenters, and those who put their author life and advice on the internet. You make me feel less alone in this endeavor. Thank you as always.
To my newly founded writer's table buds.
To you, the readers, especially those who review or make requests, this book literally wouldn't exist without those requests for more of this crew. But even if you just read, I love you all and appreciate every time you decide to take a chance on an indie like me.
And, as always and endlessly, to the person who knew every plot point before they ever made it to the page because I have been talking about this thing for two years now. And who, despite knowing every single plot point, still read through the thing (twice!) and gave advice on how to make it better. You are my ahthae and my eaahla: the most sparkling thing in my whole universe. Thanks for the mushroom pictures. Love you, B, enjoy your polyamorous aliens.

Thank You So Much For Picking
Up A Copy of
Unlicensed Delivery

For News About My Latest
Releases Sign Up To My
Mailing List At:

WillSoulsbyMcCreath.com

Or come find me on Social
Media, when I'm there I'm
@nopoodles

Enjoy my FREE Short
Stories over on
nopoodles.wordpress.com

www.ingramcontent.com/pod-product-compliance
Lightning Source LLC
Chambersburg PA
CBHW062008190726
48283CB00002BA/519